1/93

Sons of Fire

Also by Max McCoy

The Sixth Rider

Max McCoy

Sons

of

Fire

A DOUBLE D WESTERN
DOUBLEDAY
New York   London   Toronto   Sydney   Auckland

A Double D Western
published by doubleday
a division of Bantam Doubleday Dell Publishing Group, Inc.
666 Fifth Avenue, New York, New York 10103

Double D Western, Doubleday,
and the portrayal of the letters DD
are trademarks of Doubleday, a division of
Bantam Doubleday Dell Publishing Group, Inc.

Library of Congress Cataloging-in-Publication Data

McCoy, Max.
Sons of fire / Max McCoy.—1st ed.
    p.   cm.
1. United States—History—Civil War, 1861–1865—Fiction.
I. Title.
PS3563.C3523S65   1993
813'.54—dc20   92-17301
                    CIP

isbn 0-385-42030-7
Copyright © 1993 by Max McCoy
All Rights Reserved
Printed in the United States of America
January 1993
First Edition

10 9 8 7 6 5 4 3 2 1

For My Brother

Author's Note

MUCH OF WHAT FOLLOWS is true. Although the Fenn family is a product of imagination, their experience of the guerrilla war on the Missouri-Kansas border is based in fact. The depredations committed on both sides of the insurrection—from Quantrill's bloody raid on Lawrence to Ewing's desperate *Order Number Eleven*—are difficult to understand and impossible to condone. These and other acts spawned a generation of hate, bent the characters of young men such as the Younger brothers and Frank and Jesse James, and brought Missouri the undying reputation as the "Mother of Outlaws." This work is offered in celebration not of those few individuals whose hatred brought them notoriety, but to those forgotten families who were able to endure the storm, go on with their lives, and find it within themselves to forgive.

—MAX MCCOY
Lawrence, Kansas
March 1991

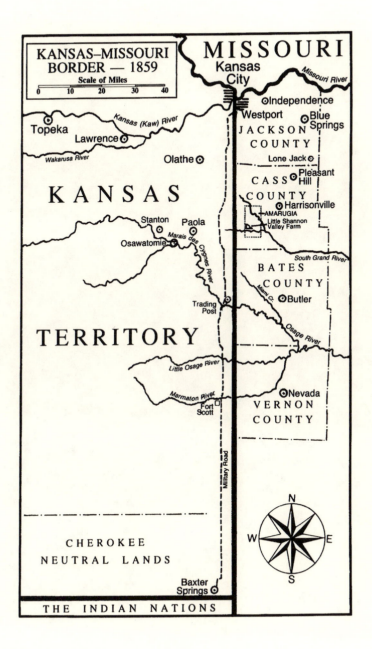

Sons of Fire

1

THE YOUNG SCHOOLMASTER stood in the doorway of the log schoolhouse, hands in his pockets. His heavy-lidded blue eyes gazed to the east, where the sun was just now clearing the horizon. The golden rays shot through the trees and were caught by a thousand ice crystals clinging to the stubble on the hard winter ground.

The youth stretched out his hand, palm out, as if to receive the warmth. Back in Ohio, he reckoned, the sun would already be a hand's width above the trees. He sighed heavily and his breath hung in the air. Not that long ago he had been a schoolboy himself, trudging across the brittle ground, his feet aching from the cold.

He stepped back and shut the door, then crossed down the row of log slab benches to the stone fireplace at the back wall. The fire had been well-banked the night before, and there were still embers to be found among the ashes. He took a stick of kindling from the box and stirred the embers about, puffing and blowing, and soon the fire sprang back to life. He added successively larger pieces of wood to the flame until, satisfied, he clapped the ash from his hands and stood.

He removed his coat and muffler and hung them from a peg. There were still a few minutes before the school day would begin, so he sat at his desk and retrieved a sheet of paper from the drawer. He rubbed his hands together to restore circulation, then uncapped the inkwell and dipped his pen.

Stanton, Kansas Territory
Dec. 3, 1859

Dearest Mother:
I pray this letter finds you well. It is a pleasant morning, this; the sun is just rising, causing the trees, bushes, and grass to glitter like brilliants, while the hanging sheets of frost drop from them, announcing his warmth, and then silently melt away. I stood in my schoolhouse door, and viewing this, it made me feel a new life, and merry as the birds. But these feelings and thoughts will soon be forgotten by the arrival of eight or ten of my scholars, who come laughing and tripping along as though their lives would always be this beautiful, calm, and serene. And I wish that I could always be as these children. But I have been so no doubt, and I have no reason to expect it a second time. Every year rings its changes and no two are alike—

The tolling of the bell in the steeple of the new stone church at Osawatomie, a few miles down the Marais des Cygnes River, made the young man pause. The bell alternated between tolling a death knell and pealing an alarm.

A pair of schoolboys came jostling through the door, all elbows and grins.

"Jason," the schoolmaster asked, "why is the Reverend Adair sounding the bell? What has happened?"

"News just came," the boy said, pulling off his rough canvas overcoat. "They hung old John Brown just before noon yesterday at Charles Town." Then he closed his eyes and proudly recited, word-for-word, a portion of the newspaper account: "No dying speech was allowed. Two thousand federal troops and cannon were on hand. John Brown thanked the jailers for their kindness, and handed over a note that said, 'I am now quite certain that the crimes of this guilty land will never be purged away, except by blood.' Then he said, 'I am ready at any time; do not keep me waiting.' His last words were, 'This is a beautiful country—I have not cast my eyes over it before.' A black cape was placed over his head and John Brown was hanged. The body swung for nearly an hour on the gibbet, in full sight of heaven and earth."

The schoolmaster nodded, and again took up his pen.

The day has started, I must now attend to my duties. Have you received the five dollars I enclosed in my last letter? I do not trust the mails. Advise me if the funds did not reach you, and I will send more. As ever, you are in my heart.

Your Son,
William C. Quantrill

2

ZACHARY FENN was the first to reach the rocky ford across the Marais des Cygnes River, and he reined the big black horse to a stop while he waited for the others to catch up. His older brothers, Frank and Patrick, riding on each side of the small herd of cattle, were just now cresting the last rise into the valley. Drawing up behind them was Uncle Fitz, driving the wagon, his .50-caliber Hawken lying on a blanket behind him.

The older boys carried .36-caliber revolving pistols in their belts, and Zachary—who was not yet seventeen but who was already bigger than most full-grown men—was armed with a double-hammered shotgun slung over his shoulder.

Even at this distance the cold winter air carried the jangle and slap of harness, the impact of shod hooves on the hard-packed ground, and the gentle lowing of the cattle to Zachary's ears. He knew he would catch hell from his brothers for ranging so far ahead, but he was impatient to cross the river. On the other side was the village of Trading Post, where they would pasture the cattle and spend a few warm hours drinking real coffee and exchanging news at the general store.

The shadows lengthened across the valley while the others caught up, and Zachary became vaguely aware of another kind of feeling besides the impatience of youth, a feeling that came from the pit of his stomach. He couldn't put the feeling into words, exactly, but it had to do with his breath that hung in clouds before him, the horse between his knees, his brothers behind him, and the river ahead. Crossing the river suddenly had more significance than just a warm fire and a full belly.

Zachary felt his life coursing through time like the water of the river, rolling between the banks, threading its way over the stones at the ford, sometimes disappearing beneath the thin sheets of ice between the rocks, but flowing steadily, unquestioningly, toward an unseen destination. The feeling spooked him, and he unslung the shotgun from his shoulder and laid it across the saddle.

They were, after all, on the old military road that ran like a saber scar down the frontier side of the border that separated the State of Missouri from Kansas Territory. This rutted ribbon was originally part of the "permanent" frontier of the 1840s, meant to forever separate whites and Indians. That idea was abandoned after large grants of land were ceded to the states following the war with Mexico and the idea of manifest destiny—one nation stretching from ocean to ocean—had taken hold. Now the road ran through the most murderous strip of ground in a region that was collectively known by the rest of the country as Bleeding Kansas. The blood flowed over the question of how far slavery would extend into the nation that appeared destined to stretch from the Atlantic to the Pacific.

Not far from where they rode, the Missourian Charles Hamelton had rounded up men who were formerly his neighbors and shot them to death in a shallow ravine, making good on a threat to exterminate abolitionist "snakes"; four years earlier, old John Brown and his sons had started the bloodshed by hacking to death five pro-slavery men along the banks of Potawatomie Creek. While the issue of whether Kansas should be admitted as a free state or a slave state dominated the emotions and manipulations of politicians back East, in the territory itself either belief—or what others thought you believed—could get you killed.

But even in the midst of insurrection, life went on; there were crops to be planted and harvested, cattle to buy and sell, families to be clothed and fed, even if it had to be under the protection of loaded guns. The Fenns, who had purchased their thirty head of cattle at Baxter Springs in the Cherokee Neutral Lands and were driving them back north to their farm just across the line in Cass County, Missouri, had been lucky so far. Not once during these years of trouble had they been forced to fire a gun in anger.

Zachary's uneasy feeling began to pass as the others neared.

"Trouble?" Frank asked as he drew abreast.

"Nope."

"Then what've you got your scattergun unlimbered for?"

"Don't know," Zachary said lamely as he slung the shotgun back over his shoulder. "Guess I thought I heard something."

"Don't get so far ahead of us again," Frank said sternly.

Zachary nudged Raven into the river, and the horse protested but broke the ice across the ford just the same. To the east and north of the river lay the mill and the village's scattered dwellings. Trading Post had originally been established in the 1820s by the French to trade with the Osage Indians, Uncle Fitz had told the boys. Part of what the traders sought was the swans that made the muddy river their home. Their feathers were prized. The name of the river, *Marais des Cygnes,* meant the marsh of swans, but like the beaver, the swans had long since been killed off.

The village that remained depended on its water-powered grist mill and what traffic that was brought by the military road—travelers such as the Fenns, for whom Trading Post was just over the halfway point between Baxter Springs and their Cass County farm.

Zachary sat upon his horse atop the creek bank and studied the community. There were three whitewashed wood-framed houses in a row, made from real lumber and not of logs, and at the end of the row was the two-story mill. Water from the river was channeled in troughs to the wheel, which drove the millstone inside. One side of the mill housed the general store and post office.

Farther down from the mill were the remnants of a log stockade built by the military in some decade past, and now long since abandoned. While Uncle Fitz hitched the team in front of the mill, the brothers drove the cattle into the fort, guiding them into a corner of the old stockade that had been boxed off by a split-rail fence to make a corral. Squatters sometimes lived in the bleak shelter of the stalls, but now, in the dead of winter, it was deserted.

"Somebody will have to stay with the stock," Frank said.

Anger caused Zachary's cheeks to flush, but he held his tongue. His older brother was meting out punishment for his impatience at crossing the river. Finally Zach simply nodded and swung down from the blood-colored bay.

"Start yourself a fire to keep you warm," Frank advised. "We'll bring you a plate of supper in a little while. Let go with one barrel of the shotgun if you smell trouble, and we'll come running."

. . . .

"Where'd you get that stock?" asked the owner of the mill, a tired-looking man named Cady who had watched from a window as the little remuda had passed.

"Baxter's Springs," Uncle Fitz replied as he eased himself onto one of the chairs surrounding the plank table and dug in the pockets of his buckskin jacket for a twist of chewing tobacco.

"They ain't been driven up the Texas Road, have they?"

"No, they been wintered in John Baxter's pasture."

"Keep them away from our stock, just the same," Cady said, not unkindly. Texas fever had spread like prairie fire from one herd to another in the past months, killing every head of stock that caught it. Although its cause was not yet understood—it would be another decade or so before the cattle tick was identified as the carrier of the disease, and a decade after that before laws would be passed to control the epidemic—folks knew it was brought by the scrawny, slat-ribbed cattle driven up from Texas and Mexico. Many believed the cattle caught the disease just by being driven, so it was also called trail fever. All stock except that which had been wintered locally was regarded with suspicion.

The boys Frank and Patrick sat down beside their uncle, and for a few cents each they got a tin plate of rabbit stew. Uncle Fitz also dug deep for a brown jug of corn liquor, and Frank reflected on how his father was right about how Fitz lived for the moment and gave no thought for tomorrow.

"This'll thaw you out," Fitz said, passing the jug to Patrick after taking a long pull himself. Patrick took a sip, and his eyes bulged as he felt the fire pour down into his belly. Frank took the jug from him and passed it on down the table, to a traveling preacher who eagerly filled his tin cup and toasted Uncle Fitz's health.

The jug then made its way along to a couple of rough-looking strangers at the end of the table. Their clothes betrayed the fact that they had been in the saddle for days, and neither had shaved in a week or more. Frank took them for kin. The older one had fists the size of hams and ruined yellow teeth, and the younger had quick darting eyes that took everything in but revealed little. They each took a swallow, the older man nodded his thanks, and the jug was returned to Uncle Fitz, where the round began once again.

Again, Frank refused to take his pull.

The circuit rider was a gaunt man with bad breath and a wreath of black hair crowning a balding pate. He introduced himself as the *Reverend* Larkin Skaggs, and as his tongue was loosened by the alcohol, he launched into an impromptu sermon on how infant damnation worked as a part of God's grand design of salvation. As he warmed to the subject he described in passionate detail how these children, along with deliberate sinners, writhed in the flames of eternal torture.

Frank knew by the look on his uncle's face that he now regretted having shared with the preacher. Such religious fervor Fitz found distasteful, and although he had not practiced his Catholicism since leaving Ireland, the fact the man was Protestant—even though his brother-in-law and nephews were, strictly speaking, Protestant as well—irritated him. He was nearly to the point of smashing the jug over the parson's head when Frank spoke up.

"Here now," Frank began in an even voice, "I am enjoying a little supper after a long day on the road and these stories of babies being roasted alive are upsetting to my digestion. I would appreciate it very kindly if you would save your lectures for a more deserving congregation."

"Surely you're not closing your ears to the word of God?" Skaggs responded, hands open in supplication, his breath rolling across the table like an Old Testament plague.

"Parson, I beg to differ with you," Frank said, placing his spoon down and looking up with blue eyes that were beginning to blaze with determination. "It is my studied belief that the word of God is revealed to each man according to his capacity to receive it. Painfully obvious to me is the fact that our capacities differ. I will thank you to keep those differences to yourself while my brother, my uncle, and I finish the supper we've paid for and that we now mean to enjoy."

Uncle Fitz and Patrick, who were sitting next to each other, exchanged grins and elbows over this last volley.

"Frank's been schooled back East," Patrick explained gleefully. "He sure can use some words, can't he? I like it when somebody gets him riled."

The reference to his Boston education annoyed Frank, because in situations it usually started a verbal argument that ended in a fistfight to prove which was the better man. Frank, twenty-three years old and blessed with the Fenn's size and strength, more often than not settled the matter.

"Surely not an intellectual," the parson said, drawing out each syllable of the word as if he were pronouncing a disease. "Have you heard tell of the horrible deaths of Thomas Paine and Voltaire? They died in agony, condemned for eternity to the fiery pits of hell."

"Have you actually read *Common Sense?*" Frank asked. "Have you read *Candide?*"

"I would not read such filth."

"He couldn't read a word of it if he tried," Cady called from where he was stacking supplies on the far side of the room. "Can't read the Good Book, neither. Can't read, it's that simple. The Reverend Skaggs finds his inspiration at the bottom of a jug."

Frank laughed.

"Being able to read the chicken scratchings of others has nothing to do with smarts," the circuit rider fumed.

"I'll grant you that, Parson," Frank said easily. "Teach a fool to read and you still have a fool. But the education of a lifetime is open to any man willing to listen and learn, and you've demonstrated your desire to do neither."

"Infidel!" the parson spat and jumped to his feet. Frank felt a momentary surge in expectation of a fight, but the pitiful man was merely retreating to sit against the wall in a far corner of the store, where he could nurse his wounds in private.

"The parson ain't as much of a fool as I thought he was," Uncle Fitz observed.

The two strangers at the table regarded Frank warily, as a fox might sniff around a baited trap. One of them sat back and folded his arms across his chest while the other leaned forward, right arm cocked on the table.

"We know how you feel about country preachers," he said smoothly. "Tell us, now, what might be your stand on the slavery question?"

3

I T WASN'T THE QUESTION so much as the man's attitude—betrayed by the forced smile and hard-set eyes, and by the bone handle of the skinning knife tucked into his belt—that disturbed Frank Fenn.

"Our stand on chattel slavery is no secret to our neighbors along the border," Frank said. "Where might you call home, and what might be your stand?"

The man's smile broke a little at the corners when he realized he had lost the advantage, but he recovered quickly.

"We're from Jackson County. I'm Jeremy Herd and this is my cousin, Jess."

No other information was offered. Frank reckoned them for mule buyers, or bounty hunters who tracked runaway slaves, or perhaps fire-eaters who had crossed the line to make some trouble. They had probably voted more times in Kansas Territorial elections than they ever had back home in Jackson County, Missouri.

"We're Missourians ourselves," Frank said easily. "We have a spread along the South Grand River in Cass County."

"So you're from the hills of Amarugia," Herd said, pronouncing the name *Am-ah-roo-gee*. "We've heard tell of strange doings in those parts, of kings and black magic and folks who are afraid to go out at night. Know anything of it?"

Frank could feel the parson's eyes burning on the back of his neck.

"Everybody's afraid to go out at night these days," Frank said. "All we know is corn, wheat, livestock. Some hogs and sorghum, those things it takes to make a living. We're farmers, not one of the hill folk, and we don't have any truck with backwoods kingdoms. We live and let live, friend."

"Is that what you say about slavery as well?"

Frank's easy smile came back.

"We hold with the law. If a man wants to keep slaves, that's his business, not ours," Frank said. As he spoke he slipped his right hand into his coat pocket and touched a small clasp wallet that held a daguerreotype, and he silently prayed for forgiveness.

"I knowed by the look that you was all right," Herd said. "Say, you haven't seen any niggers on the way up from the neutral lands, have you? We're hunting a big buck that escaped from the widow Garner place at Harrisonville."

"No," Frank said slowly, "we haven't seen any runaways."

"See there?" Jess asked. "I knew he didn't come this far south, not with that lame foot of his."

"Damn," Jeremy Herd said. "I thought he might have made for one of the Yankee homes around here. The black bastard has probably gone and froze himself to death in some ditch. We may have come a long way for nothin'."

"I'd keep that kind of talk under my hat, lads," Uncle Fitz said, joining the conversation in a conspiratorily low voice. "We ain't exactly in the heart of Dixie."

The strangers nodded. The matter was over. Even so, Frank's uneasiness remained. He lapsed into silence and his brow became furrowed in thought.

Zachary Fenn sat cross-legged in front of the fire, a buffalo robe draped over his shoulders and the shotgun across his lap. The sky was clear and the stars shone bright and hard above, and to the east the full moon was rising over the river. The stock had settled in for the night and there wasn't a thing left to do but wait.

Zachary didn't mind being alone because it gave him time to think, and his thinking always seemed clearer when it was done under an open sky. A roof and walls made it hard for a body to breathe, and seemed to hem in the spirit as well. Small spaces made for small thoughts, Uncle Fitz always said, but the open canopy of the sky was a fitting canvas for the imagination.

Zachary thought mostly about things which others boys of his age and circumstances thought about: horses and dogs and hunting and, of course, women. Of the latter he and his brother, Patrick, knew some, but not all, thanks to the Barriclaw sisters up on Owens Creek.

But sometimes he thought of the stories and poetry which Uncle Fitz often recited, some of which had stayed with Fitz from the days of his youth, and others which he had read during the long winters in the mountains. From Fitz he heard of the romances of Sir Walter Scott, Mallory's Arthurian saga, and other tales.

At other times Zachary found himself pondering things that had no answer, or at least no answer likely to easily be put into words.

What, for example, was the meaning of a life? Not life itself, but a single life, an individual. It was easy to see how generals and presidents fit into the scheme of things, but what of common folk like the Fenns? It seemed it hardly made a difference whether they lived or died, at least the way most folks reckoned things. Certainly the generals and presidents wouldn't give their passing a second thought. Men were supposed to die for their country when it was necessary, weren't they?

That would be square with me if I was the one to decide when it was necessary, Zachary thought.

What would it be like after they were dead? Zachary couldn't imagine it, no more than he could imagine what it was like before he was born. He had heard enough from the circuit riders to know they didn't have the answer, and probably never would. He didn't know enough about his mother's religion even to guess. But he allowed that John Baxter, the Universalist minister they had purchased the stock from, might be on the right track.

Baxter had spoken of the ultimate force in the universe as being love, and how there wasn't no hell at all below, but that the ultimate hell is being shut off from that universal love. Zachary had asked that, if hell didn't exist, did that mean there was no heaven either?

"What do *you* think, boy?" Baxter had asked.

Zachary still didn't have an answer, but he turned the matter over in his mind as he lay back against the log and gazed into the fire. He liked the idea of there not being a hell, no eternal flames to torment sinners—how could a loving God stand to roast his children, no matter how badly they had behaved? The idea there might not be a heaven, either, disturbed him. Not so much for his own sake—at seventeen life itself seemed eternal—but for his mother's. She had died when he was eleven, and he found comfort in the thought that she waited in heaven, and that someday they would be reunited.

The sound of something moving down the path to the river drew his mind back to the present. He scooted into the shadows, out of the circle of firelight, and waited.

Presently the sound grew nearer, and he could tell from the rhythm that it was someone walking, someone walking and humming and the creak and clank of what sounded like a bucket. Through the brush he could catch glimpses, a patch of silver here, a piece of fabric there, but it wasn't until she emerged in the clearing that he saw her fully.

The girl appeared to be Zachary's age or a little older, with pale skin and straight blond hair that shone white in the moonlight. She was wearing a calico dress and a heavy shawl was thrown around her shoulders. She was humming an old fiddle tune. A water bucket dangled from her left hand, and she stopped dead when she caught the glint of firelight from the barrel of Zachary's shotgun.

"Who's there?" she asked, and her shoulders began to tremble.

Zachary started to say something, but stopped himself because he didn't know what to say without frightening her more. Maybe he should just let her pass. But there was something about her, something that made it painful for Zachary to let her go.

"My brother is right behind me," she said. "And he's got his meat rifle with him."

She was turning to run when Zachary spoke up.

"Wait," he said simply, stepping forward. Even in this light Zachary could see that her eyes were pale and extraordinarily beautiful. "Don't go . . . I mean, you can go if you like, but I ain't going to hurt you none. Go ahead and get your water."

"Who are you?"

Zachary told her, and added: "My brothers left me here to guard the stock. That's why I've got this shotgun." He leaned the barrel against the trunk of a tree. "I didn't mean to scare you. I hid because I didn't know what you might have been, either. I'm sorry."

She nodded, a little more relaxed now, but still unsure of herself. She knew she ought to get back to the house, but she loved talking with strangers. Finally, her curiosity won out over her caution.

"My name is Sarah Drake," she said. "My family lives in the last house in the row above. We moved out here from Ohio two years ago. We're Friends."

"Friends?" Zachary asked.

"You know, Quakers," she said.

"Oh."

"Our pa died last year."

"I'm sorry."

"I miss him so. It's lonely out here, and he used to tell me stories— Say, do you know any stories?"

"I reckon I know a few," Zachary said. "What kind of stories do you like?"

"All kinds," she said. "Could you come up to the house, then? Sit in front of the fire and tell me a story? I can't stay here with you, you know. It's not—"

"You'd freeze, for one thing," Zachary said. "You're not dressed for this kind of weather. Besides, I have to wait here for my brothers. They're up at the mill, and I can't leave the stock."

"I understand," she said. "I'd better get the water now. Ma will be expecting me back." But she stood there a few moments longer before turning toward the river.

Presently she was back, carrying a full bucket. She stopped in the clearing and called to Zachary.

"Say," she said, "Would you like to come up to the house for a cup of cider when your brothers get back?"

The Drake cabin was so small that Zachary wondered how the family of three could live without constantly bumping into one another. All of their meals were cooked in the fireplace and eaten at a plank table near the door. The mother slept on the bed downstairs and Sarah and her brother, Amos, had separate beds in lofts tucked under the eaves at either end.

The presence of Zachary and Uncle Fitz seemed to fill the cabin to bursting. Mother Drake regarded them warily at first, and quizzed them about the family and their connections in Cass County. She was somewhat appalled that her seventeen-year-old daughter would invite strangers into the home without asking first, but the more she talked with Zachary and his uncle—who had insisted on accompanying the lad for caution's sake—the brighter she became. She, too, was hungry for conversation, and the pair seemed honest and straightforward enough; in addition, the boy was polite and the uncle was well-read and possessed a puckish Irish charm.

They drank warm cider by the fire and talked politely of nothing in particular: the weather, the crops, how different things were back in Ohio. Soon the talk turned to the trouble along the border and the slavery question.

Mother Drake allowed that they were neither abolitionists nor Southern sympathizers; slavery was morally wrong, but they could not endorse the belief that bloodshed was necessary to correct the problem. Killing was repugnant, she said, no matter how worthy the ideal was that pulled the trigger.

It was the Friends belief that the United States should follow the example set by the British Empire. In 1833, Parliament provided for the emancipation of nearly a million black slaves in the West Indies. The slave owners received compensation from the government, and the slaves themselves were freed following a period of apprenticeship. By 1850, the process was complete and slaves in all British possessions had been set free.

"That is the sane approach to things," Uncle Fitz said, "but I'm afraid there is a blood lust over the land, and nothing but war will satisfy it. The trouble may have started here, but it will spread—"

"Please, no more politics," Sarah pleaded. "I was promised a story. I hate Kansas. I want to hear about something romantic, something from a long time ago and far away."

"Sarah, don't be rude," Mother Drake warned. "These are guests."

"No, it's all right," Fitz said, laughing. "She is quite right. It is time for a story. Something romantic, she says, from a long time ago and far away. Which one shall we tell?"

"I am somewhat partial to the Tale of the Dark Rider," Zachary said.

"The very one! Good choice, lad. Have you ever heard it, girl?"

"No," Sarah said.

"All right, then. I will begin."

Uncle Fitz took a last drink of cider and fixed his gaze upon Sarah, who was sitting on the floor. She smoothed her dress and looked up at him, eyes bright with anticipation.

"You must understand this took place in Ireland, where I grew up, which is indeed far away. And it took place a long time ago, but the story was passed down from generation to generation, so that we might not forget; I heard it first from my own father, who heard it from his father, and so forth. It is a tale of true love, and true love must never be forgotten. Before I begin, you must promise me that you will tell it to your own children some-day."

"But I'm not even married," Sarah protested.

"Ah, but you will be. And it will be a lucky rascal who wins your favor and is allowed to gaze into those eyes of yours every day."

Sarah blushed.

"All right," she said. "I promise."

"Good," Fitz said, and winked at Zachary. "Now, in those dark days in which our story takes place, Ireland was under the heel of Cromwell. You have heard of Cromwell, the so-called Lord Protector? After crushing armies loyal to Charles Stuart, Cromwell ruled with an iron fist, and took land away from the rightful own-ers and gave it to his friends.

"A true Irishman could not own land, he could not even rent. Families were cast out into the darkness, to survive as they could. Those who resisted were crushed, and the land was red with blood.

"Now, in those times there was a family that lived in our village whose father had been killed in the fight to replace Charles Stuart on the throne. They lost the ancestral home and were forced to live in the countryside like animals. They fought for every scrap of food and sought shelter wherever they could find it—in huts, or stables, even in caves. The mother soon died from this kind of harsh exposure, leaving an only son and two little sisters, who were not long for this world, either.

"The boy's name was Seamus, and he resolved to become a robber and thief—a highwayman, a sort of pirate who stalks the land and not the sea—before he would allow his sisters to starve to death. So one night when the moon was full he waited on the King's Road until an unlucky Englishman chanced by, and he fell upon him with his bare hands, and fought like a demon. This poor Englishman lost his sword and his horse and all of his gold, and barely escaped with his life.

"Seamus bought food and warm clothes for his sisters, but of course in time the food ran out and he returned to the highway during the full moon, but now with a sword and a horse and eventually a brace of pistols taken from one of the victims. He began to wear black from head to toe, and cloaked himself in a swirling black cape.

"Soon it became known that the King's Highway was haunted by an Irish ghost seeking revenge, and that to travel the road by moonlight was to risk one's life. Of course, nothing could fill the emptiness that was left by the loss of his parents, and Seamus continued to haunt the road long after his sisters were more than provided for.

"Cromwell's men began patrolling the highway, and one night Seamus killed to keep from being captured. Soon killing became a way of life for poor Seamus, and although he never killed without provocation, his sorrow and his rage nearly drove him mad. He even began to taunt the soldiers by strapping harness bells to his horse's bridle, and the soldiers were filled with dread every time they heard bells in the shadows along the road.

"One night he stopped a coach and, after knocking the driver unconscious with the flat of his sword, discovered its only occupant to be a particularly beautiful young girl. She was just arrived from England, the only daughter of the lord who had taken Seamus's family home. She wept when she saw the torment in his eyes, and Seamus could not bring himself to rob her. He loved her from the first moment he laid eyes on her, and she, him; but she was promised to another, and he carried the penalty of death upon his head. He begged her forgiveness, and rode off into the night, bells jingling.

"But he could not forget the way her face glowed in the moonlight, and his heart, which had been hardened by the labors of war, began to soften, and then to melt, and soon he found joy in merely the thought of her. So he came to her, in the night, stealing into the great house that once was his, and he woke her with a kiss.

"He vanished with the dawn.

"The girl was to be wed that day, but her heart being true, she refused and declared her love for the highwayman; her father the lord was filled with rage, and he swore vengeance on the one who had stolen the heart of his only daughter. He doubled the patrols along the highway, and kept his daughter under constant watch.

Even so, the highwayman somehow managed to see her, a whispered word here in the shadows, a secret kiss yonder in the darkness.

"The daughter, who loved both the father and the highwayman, was filled with torment. The lord pressed her relentlessly on where and when they would next meet, and swore that her highwayman would not be harmed if only they could catch him. But if she would not help, he surely would be put to death. So at last she yielded, and said they were to meet upon the highway beneath the next full moon.

"The English lord laid his plans well. As young Seamus emerged from the shadows, harness bells tinkling, to greet his love, the soldiers sprang out and seized him. Through a veil of tears the girl begged the highwayman to believe that she had betrayed him only in hopes of saving his life.

"The highwayman was hung, of course, but before he swung he forgave the girl, and counted himself among the blessed for having spent even one hour in her arms.

"The girl was inconsolable, and wasted away at an alarming pace; nothing her father could do would ease her pain nor encourage her to live. He saw that by using her love to trap the highwayman, he had forfeited his daughter's life as well. Finally merciful death came to her, and in his grief the English lord sought to comfort her in the only way he could, and that was to bury the daughter beside young Seamus.

"At night, along the King's Highway, when the moon is full and the wind is still, if you close your eyes you can hear the harness bells of the highwayman as he searches, searches, forever searches, for one last rendezvous with the daughter of the English lord."

Uncle Fitz paused for a moment, then said, "And that is the tale. Did you like it?"

"Yes," Sarah said, glancing away. Her eyes were moist with tears. "But it was so sad, I can't hardly stand it."

"The best tales usually are," Fitz said.

"Is it true?" she asked. "Did it really happen that way?"

"Aye, girl, it's as true as anything in this life is likely to be. I've heard the bells myself often enough, when I was young. But we must beg your pardon, it's getting late and Zachary's brothers will be wondering what happened to us. Thank you for the cider and the warm fire."

"Will you both come back? You have more stories to tell, don't you? I mean, when you have business about and it's not inconvenient?" Sarah asked.

"I'll be back," Zachary said.

"Of course we will," Fitz said. "It's a rare thing to have friends along the road, and it's something we won't neglect. And a sympathetic ear is something no wandering Irishman can resist."

Frank Fenn lay on his side near the fire. It was Frank's turn to watch over the stock while the others slept, and there were still a couple of hours remaining before dawn. He had seen or heard nothing, except for the passing of the Herd cousins and their pack of bloodhounds as they took the military road to the north. Like all good hunters, the Herds preferred an early start. Frank thought of the medieval legend of the Wild Huntsman, who was condemned to hunt forever with a pack of spectral dogs as punishment for violating the Sabbath.

Thinking of the Herds sparked a twinge of conscience, and Frank withdrew the daguerreotype case from his coat pocket and opened it. He turned it to catch the light from the fire. In the photograph Jenny appeared serious and somewhat stern, her dark hair drawn back into a bun and her hands resting on a Bible in her lap. He had looked at the photograph a thousand times since returning home from Boston last year. He thought of the scores of letters they had exchanged during their courtship. How different his Yankee girl would find life here, he thought. How different.

And, he wondered, would she find him different as well? He feared that the ideals and spiritual convictions they shared had been compromised by the necessities of life on the border. Talk was cheap, and real conviction could only be demonstrated through action. Why didn't he stand up to the bounty hunters at the mill? It was easy to tell himself that discretion was the best policy, that there were his brothers and uncle to consider, that the job at hand was to get the stock home.

But the question remained, lurking in the dark corners of his heart, gathered in the pit of his stomach: Was Frank Fenn a coward? He tried to ignore it, but it refused to go away, when dawn came at last it was still with him. He knew with dread certainty that it was something that only action, and not thought, could answer.

4

THE NEGRO burst from the woods and stumbled onto the road, caught his ankle on one of the frozen ruts and went down hard just a few yards ahead of the wagon. The team reared and Frank Fenn had to put his back and shoulders against the reins to turn the horses in time to prevent the black man from being crushed beneath their hooves.

Uncle Fitz, who was riding beside his nephew, instinctively reached behind with his right hand and brought up his old brown-barreled Hawken from the bed of the wagon, all without taking his eyes from the road. The racket from a pack of hounds being run hard was getting louder, and even though it was winter the hardwood thicket was so dense they could not yet be seen.

The boys were up ahead with the stock, and Frank's horse—which had thrown a shoe just after they had left the military road and turned east, toward Missouri—was tied to the back of the wagon.

Fitz thumbed the hammer back on the mountain rifle.

The negro lay with the side of his head on the road and his arms spread before him. He watched Fitz cock the rifle and closed his eyes in despair. His shirt and breeches were rags, his hands and arms and legs were covered with mud and sweat and laced by dozens of briar cuts, and his bare feet were swollen and bloody. His left foot, which he had caught in the wagon rut, was bent at an unnatural angle away from his ankle.

"I ain't fixing to shoot you," Fitz said, and craned his neck to peer into the woods. "But I can't vouch for them that's chasing you. Where'd you run away from?"

The man was silent.

"Where you running to, then?"

"Mister James H. Lane's house at Lawrence."

"You got a fur piece to go," Fitz said. "You're still on the Missouri side. I reckon you got about one minute to decide whether you're going to lay there in the middle of the road and let them hounds get to you, or be on your way. It don't make no difference to me which you choose."

"I think my ankle's busted."

"I am truly sorry to hear that, but this is none of our business," Fitz said, and spat tobacco juice on the ground. "We'd best be on our way. Let's go, Frankie."

"We can't leave him like this," Frank Fenn said, finding his voice at last, and the declaration surprised him as much as it did his Uncle Fitz.

"Get in the back of the wagon," Frank Fenn told the black man.

"What in thunder is wrong with you?" Fitz demanded. "Are you trying to get us killed? Do you know what kind of men track runaway slaves? I've been in plenty of tight spots in the mountains when redskins wanted my hair, but I think I'd rather face a full-dress Crow war party than try to take a prize buck away from a gang of bounty hunters."

"It's not right to leave him here," Frank Fenn said resolutely. "Do you know what they do to runaways? We can argue about it later, Uncle Fitz, but I'm asking you to stick by me on this one."

Fitz spat on the ground in disgust.

"If you weren't blood, I'd brain you myself," he said.

Frank handed the reins to his uncle, climbed down from the wagon, and helped the negro to his feet. He gave a shoulder as the black man limped to the back of the flatbed, where he lay down among the supplies. "Thank you, mister," the man said as Frank threw a canvas tarp over him.

Frank pulled himself back up to the seat, took the reins, and nudged the team forward. The wagon started with a lurch and a clatter, and the man hiding in the back had to bite his lip to keep from crying out from the pain in his foot.

The wagon was hardly fifty yards away when the pack of bloodhounds swarmed onto the road, followed by two heavyset men in thick fur coats. They both wore heavy revolvers, and the bigger one had a bone-handled skinning knife tucked into his wide leather belt. Frank started to turn his head to look, but Fitz cautioned him to keep looking straight ahead.

"It's them all right," Fitz said. "The Herd cousins."

The hounds swarmed around the spot where the negro had fallen, but milled aimlessly when the trail ended close by. The bounty hunters cursed and looked down the road, eyeing the wagon suspiciously.

"You in the wagon!" shouted Jeremy Herd, the bigger of the two, as he stood with his feet apart in the middle of the road. "Stop! You got our nigger in there?"

Fitz turned and cupped his hand to his ear. The Hawken was still across his lap, unseen by the bounty hunters.

"What?"

"Damn you, have you got our nigger?"

"Ain't seen no niggers," Fitz shouted back with a shrug.

The wagon was a hundred yards away.

"Lying bastard," Jeremy Herd said.

"Maybe they're tellin' the truth," Jess offered.

"Them dogs don't lie," Jeremy said. "The trail ends here and there was only one place for our boy to go. Mark that wagon with the kid and the old buzzard beside him. We met them at Trading Post. What was the name?"

"Fenn."

"That's it. We can't catch up with them now, seeing as how we're on foot, but we'll run into them one day soon. Then we'll settle the score over them stealing our nigger to claim the two-hundred-dollar reward for themselves."

5

SHADOWS WERE LONG on the winter ground by the time the wagon drew up the path that led to the big two-story cabin on the hill. Smoke curled lazily from the huge stone chimney, which stood like a sentinel against the evening sky. A blue haze covered the valley that separated the farm from the rolling hills to the east—Amarugia—where distant fires winked. Frank Fenn eased the team to a stop around back, near the kitchen door, and handed the reins to his uncle.

The evening was so still that the pop of canvas sounded unreal as Frank flipped back the tarp. The black man had lapsed into merciful unconsciousness. Although the fugitive was well over six feet and weighed two hundred and fifty pounds, Frank shouldered the limp figure as easily as someone else might pick up a child, and with sure steps made his way to the door. The sounds of talking and laughter, and the aromas of cornbread and ham, were reassuring. He lifted the latch with one hand and eased his way, sideways and stooping, through the door into the well-lit kitchen.

The man sitting at the broad table fell silent, and the girl who was at the sideboard stirring a pot of beans dropped her spoon. Francis Fenn stood stiffly in the doorway, and the weight of the black man on his shoulders grew heavier. Words alone seemed woefully incapable of explaining the situation.

"He's hurt," fifteen-year-old Caitlin Fenn said finally, with the authority of the only woman in a household of five men. "I'll make a pallet in front of the fireplace in the big room where it's warm, and we can see about cleaning him up." She smoothed her apron and, as she knelt to pick her spoon from the floor, she glanced up at her father.

Francis Fenn nodded.

"Go on, Frank," he said.

Caitlin went to get the blankets, the wash basin, and the rags, while Frank carried the fugitive through the kitchen. Patrick and Zachary Fenn, who had just returned from pasturing the stock in near the river, burst through the door to ask who or what Frank had carried into the house.

"Let me worry about it," Francis Fenn said, then added, "Truth is, I haven't found out myself. You boys help your Uncle Fitzhugh put up the team. When you're done with that you can finish putting supper on the table. I reckon Caitlin will be busy for a spell. Oh, and Patrick—"

"Yes, sir?"

"Make sure the gate is secured on the far corral. I don't want that cattle to get near the rest of the stock until we're sure they ain't got the fever."

"It's secure," Patrick said. "We just came from there."

"Check it again. We have to be sure."

Francis Fenn sucked on his pipe and, amid a wreath of curling smoke, studied his daughter's face in the flickering light thrown from the hearth. Her brow was tight with concentration as she sat on a stool and mended her brother's clothes. Her expression was so like that of their mother that Francis had to glance away to keep the water from his eyes. Seven years had passed since cholera had taken Mary Fitzhugh Fenn and her body was laid in the side of a hill a few hundred yards from the house, but Francis Fenn felt the blade of loss as sharply as if it had struck yesterday.

For a moment, he was by that lonely hillside grave beside the big oak, thinking once more of how radically his love had altered the course of her life, how it had brought her at last to be buried alone in strange soil so far away from her family home. Ireland seemed so long ago and far away that it was like a dream, a dream both bright with pleasure and dark with fear.

It startled him to realize that Caitlin was now Mary's age, just shy of her sixteenth birthday, when they were married. Oh, the scandal it had caused. He was Scotch Irish—Protestant—and her family was devoutly Roman Catholic. Her kin, with the exception of her devoted little brother Liam Fitzhugh, had disowned her. Taking Liam with them, they booked passage to America, and settled with other Irish immigrants near Mount Sterling, Kentucky.

She gave him Little Frank the next year, and they sharecropped in Kentucky for the next ten years, until the Mexican War came and he enlisted in the army out of a sense of duty to his new country. This had caused a bitter argument with Liam, by then twenty-three, who regarded the conflict as none of their business. It was the rich and powerful, Liam argued, that profited from war—never the common folk. But Big Francis's Protestant values could not be shaken, and Francis Fenn Sr. was with Zachary Taylor as he crossed the river and took Matamoros. Liam struck out on his own, determined to escape the influence of kings and presidents. In St. Louis he bought a rifle and other supplies, and left the states by way of the Missouri River to join the fur trade.

During his years in the mountains Liam Fitzhugh faced as many, if not more, battles than his brother-in-law had with Zachary Taylor, but at least they were his own fights. He often said the iron trade point he carried near the base of his spine was all his, while the musket ball that found its mark in Francis Fenn's shoulder at Monterrey was the result of a pissing contest between presidents on either side of the Rio Grande.

After being mustered out in 1847, Francis Fenn—who had contracted America's contagion for real estate—moved his growing family west to Cass County, Missouri. He laid claim to a spot in the fertile valley of the South Grand River, amid rolling hills that reminded him of home. Before the first spade of earth was turned, he christened the location the Little Shannon Valley. He built a small cabin, cleared a few acres, and began planting crops. They were reunited with Liam a few years later—Liam first learned of the whereabouts of his American family by word of mouth following a three-day drunk at Westport, on the Missouri River.

Although Liam was capable of a prodigious amount of work when necessary, and helped Francis Fenn build the rough-hewn, two-story house in which they now lived, he was incapable of staying in any one spot too long. So he came and he went at will, returning to his mountain haunts—and, some said, an Indian wife

—for months or as much as a year at a time, until the popularity of silk instead of beaver for hats finally put an end to the livelihood of the free trapper.

Francis Fenn tolerated the irresponsibility, and frequent insobriety, of his brother-in-law because, among all her family, Liam was the one that had stood by the marriage. Liam understood the ways of the heart. And in his own way, Liam was as grief-stricken as Francis the day he returned from the mountains in the spring of 1832 and learned of Mary's death—which occurred without benefit of priest or sacrament of the last rite.

But Liam took comfort in the children Mary had left: Frank Jr., who was a man by the time he returned from his last rendezvous in the mountains, the scamps Patrick and Zachary—named for Patrick Henry and Zachary Taylor—and little Caitlin, whom Mary had named after the mother she hadn't seen for more than half her life. Mary was thirty-two when they put her in the ground.

Liam approved of the spot that Francis Fenn had picked for her grave, because it reminded him of the tree at a secret spot where he and Mary had often played as children. The brothers-in-law also had an understanding that when their times came they would be placed beside Mary, so that she would not lie alone forever. A split-rail fence eventually went up around the grave, large enough to accommodate a family plot. At length Francis Fenn came to believe that neither money nor titles bought land and made it a family's own, but the blood of those you love.

Francis discovered the pipe had grown cold during his reflections. He leaned forward in his chair and tapped the ashes out in the hearth, glancing at the prone figure resting on the makeshift bed Caitlin had prepared. Sensing that someone was watching, the fugitive opened his eyes and caught the elder Fenn's not unkind stare.

"What will you be doing with me?" the slave asked softly.

"I don't know. We'll have to chew this thing a little finer, amongst all of us. I reckon there's a reward involved, but there's more to it than that. What's your name?"

The black man thought a moment before he answered. They had sheltered him, dressed his wounds, and fed him; they deserved nothing less than the truth.

"Ben," he said.

"Where'd you run away from?"

"The widow Garner's place in Harrisonville. I been gone three days. I've heard tell that Mister James H. Lane of Lawrence, Kansas Territory, has helped some of our kind follow the drinkin' gourd to the land up north. Do you know him?"

"I know of him," Fenn said, repacking his pipe and lighting it. "Lane is a violent abolitionist in command of a ragtag army of freestaters. It is my opinion that, regardless of his beliefs, he is as violent a man and is as responsible for as much of the bloodshed as the pro-slavery trash that crosses the border. But you are right; he has helped some niggers escape to Canada."

"Will you take me to him?"

"I don't know. To do so would be risking the safety of my family and this farm, and however I feel about chattel slavery, my blood and this land comes first. You are free to spend the night, but I can make no promises after the sun rises. We have already committed a crime by taking you in."

"I thank you, mister."

Francis Fenn stood, but turned back to ask one last question.

"Tell me," he said, "why did you run? Surely the widow Garner could not have treated you all that badly. You had plenty to eat and a dry place to sleep, did you not? You were better off than many white people who work for slave wages in factories in the East."

"Wouldn't you have run?" Ben asked, his nostrils flaring. "Wouldn't you have run if they sold your wife to a man who whipped her until she couldn't walk because she wouldn't share the corncrib they call a bed? Wouldn't you have run if they took your baby son and auctioned him off when he was old enough to roll a hogshead of tobacco? I run twice before, mister, trying to find them. They caught me each time and the widow Garner let them whack off part of my foot with an ax, not enough to keep me from walkin'—or workin'. But if they catch me this time I'll run again, even if they chop off my hands and my feet. I'll keep runnin' until there ain't nothin' left of me and the Lord calls me to the Promised Land."

The father nodded. He asked Caitlin to put some coffee on to boil and then to assemble the boys in the kitchen. Hard decisions had to be made. She nodded and put her sewing basket aside.

.   .   .   .

Francis Fenn sat at one end of the long oak table in the kitchen, and Uncle Fitz sat at the other. The boys—Frank, Patrick, and Zachary—were arranged according to rank, with Frank closest to their father. Caitlin sat apart, an embroidery hoop and needle in her hands.

"Well, what do we do with him?" Francis Fenn asked his family. Although all important decisions about the farm always rested with their pa, the children understood that each could have their say without fear of reprisal. Fenn had grown gentler toward his children following Mary's death. Allowing them to participate in the decision-making process was his way of showing them how to run a farm and a family.

"I know we can't risk keeping him here," Frank said, feeling obligated to speak first because it was his action that created the situation. "But I don't think it would be right to leave him to the mercy of the bounty hunters."

"He's someone else's property," Francis said. "If we interfere it would be like somebody taking one of our horses or cows, one of the animals we need to run this farm. Do you think that's right?"

"What you say is true, according to the law," Frank said carefully, "but I believe there is a higher law involved here—God's law. Jenny and I have spoken of this often, and I believe she is right. What we're talking about does not involve a horse or a cow, or any kind of animal at all; it's about owning another human being, with feelings and emotions the same as us."

"Are you saying niggers is as good as we are?" Fitz asked.

Frank studied the surface of the table before he answered.

"I . . . I don't know," he said. "But I know they think and feel and bleed, same as us. They have families and care about their children, same as us. Back East, there are free black men who work and dress and act like we do, with the only difference being the color of their skin. We ought to help him get to Jim Lane's house."

"We ain't in no Yankee commonwealth back East," Francis said. "This here is Missouri, and whether you like it or not people have the right to own slaves. It's illegal to help them escape. Hell, the bounty hunters even have the legal right to roust us out of bed at night and make us help them hunt a slave down. I know you did what you thought you had to do, Frank, according to your conscience. But you're responsible for more than just yourself. You have this family to think about. And if you or I or any one of us is put in jail, the rest will have to pay for it by taking up the slack. You know how things are for us right now; something like that could be the ruin of this place."

"I know, Pa."

"Boys, what do you think?"

"I think it was none of our business in the first place, of course," Patrick said before Zachary could collect his thoughts. "But all that's water under the bridge now, and we have to make the best of the situation."

Patrick paused and laid his hands palm-down on the table, as if he were touching the problem itself. Then he cocked his head and looked at his Uncle Fitz.

"Pa is right about the delicate situation we're in. We're breaking the law, no doubt about it. And I'll also allow as how Frank could be on to something, too, but those issues ain't for us to decide— Lord knows the learned gentlemen in Congress have tried for years without getting anywhere but compromised. It also strikes me that we ought to do what the Good Book says, the part about giving up to Caesar what is his. This nigger is somebody else's property; we may not all agree that's a good thing, but that's the bald fact of the matter. If we hide him or help him escape, we're committing a crime. But if we return him to where he rightfully belongs, why, not only are we doin' what's right according to the laws of God and man, but we're also going to gather us a reward —those bounty hunters weren't chasing that nigger for fun, you know. And that reward sure would help us get through the winter."

"Now there's a smart lad," Uncle Fitz said, slapping his thigh.

Frank's eyes were ablaze as he pointed his finger at Patrick and began to scold him for perverted reasoning, but his father laid a hand on his arm and urged him to hush.

"We haven't heard from everybody yet," Francis Fenn said. "Zachary, what do you think?"

"I don't know," Zachary said, brushing his blond hair away from his eyes. "I can see Frank's point, that there may be a higher law, but it scares me to think what might happen if we don't turn him in. Then I think, if Frank's right about them being the same as us, how would I feel if it was Frank or Pat or even Caitlin who was in the same fix and nobody would help them. I just can't get it straight in my mind."

"So it'd be all right with you if we was to turn him in," Patrick said.

"No, I'm not saying that at all. I'm saying I don't know."

"That's fine, Zach," Francis said. "I appreciate you being honest with us and not taking sides if you're not sure. Caitlin, my girl, what do you feel is the right thing to do?"

Caitlin kept her eyes on her sewing as she spoke.

"I agree with Frank," she said, "but not for the same reasons, because I haven't been to school and I'm not nearly as smart as he is. I don't know whether it's right or wrong to own slaves, but I'm not inclined to believe a Yankee opinion on anything.

"But let's say we were talking about a horse instead of a slave. Would it feel right to you to return that horse to an owner who beat it and lopped off part of its hoof so it couldn't run from the beatings? I don't think you would, Pa. I think you'd let that horse wander free rather than take it back to somebody who treated animals like that. I say we take him across the border and let him free."

"So you all are pretty well divided up," Francis Fenn said. "Frank and Caitlin say we take him over to Kansas Territory. Patrick and his Uncle Fitz say we turn him in and keep the reward for ourselves. And Zachary is undecided."

"Yes," Caitlin said, knotting a thread and biting it off close to the work. "But what's important is what you think, Papa. What are you going to decide?"

Francis Fenn drummed his fingers on the table and wished, not for the first and certainly not for the last time, that Mary was there to help him.

"I don't know yet, child," he said. "But I'll pray tonight and will know in the morning."

Francis Fenn was most troubled by the secret the family now had to protect—a secret that was bound to cause problems if it got out. No matter how you sliced it, it was likely to rub somebody the wrong way.

6

WHAT'S THE MATTER, Pa?" Patrick asked as he pulled up his suspenders and took a seat at the table. The boy knew something was up because none of the others lifted their eyes in greeting as he came in for breakfast.

"The new stock got out of far pasture last night," Francis Fenn said. "Found some of them up near the barn this morning. Somebody must have left the gate open."

"But I'm sure it was closed," Patrick said.

"Did you check it like I asked?"

"It was closed."

"Did you check?"

"I didn't have to," Patrick said. "I knew it was closed after me and Zachary put 'em in yesterday. Ain't that right, Zach?"

"I don't remember," Zachary said.

"He was with me," Patrick protested. "Why ain't he in trouble, too?"

"You're the one I asked to check on it," Francis Fenn said. "Besides that, you're two years older than Zachary is. You were in charge."

"This ain't fair," Patrick said. "Somebody must have come and opened the gate during the night, because I'm pretty sure it was closed the last time I saw it."

"Pretty sure isn't good enough, not if those cows are sick and infect the rest of the stock," his father said. "We were taking a risk by buying more cattle, and we talked about it beforehand, and decided the risk was acceptable if we could keep the new stock away from the rest until we were sure they didn't have the fever.

The only thing we can do now is wait and see. I have to tell you, son, I'm sorely disappointed with you."

Patrick laid his chin on his chest and clenched his eyes shut. Shame burned in his chest. He had disappointed Pa again, just like the time he had left the squirrel rifle too close to the cook fire last summer and burned off half the stock, or the time before that when he lied about stealing Zach's case knife. If only he had checked, like his father had asked. If only . . .

"It won't happen again, Pa."

"I know it won't. Next time, I'll trust Zach."

At seven o'clock that morning Frank Fenn and his father started loading the wagon with a variety of items, as if they were bound for one of their neighbors' places to do some trading: blankets, a keg of nails, some tanned hides, a hatchet, two hundred-pound sacks of grain. The last item to be placed on board was a large hoop barrel. They lifted it carefully from the ground and onto its side, to ride securely between the blankets and the grain sacks. Inside was the runaway slave that Frank had brought home.

Francis Fenn's decision was simple: it was Frank's responsibility to get Ben across the line and headed in the direction of Lawrence, as quickly and discreetly as possible. That was all the help they could afford to offer. If there was trouble, Frank was to give up the slave peaceably and let on that he had been attempting to collect the reward himself. Frank had asked for one of the .36-caliber Navy revolvers, but his father said it was too much to risk —he didn't want shooting of any kind, if it came down to it.

"You're sure you are pointin' me toward Lawrence?" Ben had asked before the lid was tacked shut.

"There wouldn't be any need to hide you if we was headed for Harrisonville," Frank said. "You just stay in here, no matter what happens. Keep buttoned up and don't come out for nothing."

Frank said goodbye to his father and swung up into the seat of the wagon. Francis Fenn tried to hide his anxiety, but he could not. His face was flushed red and his eyes were bright.

"Don't worry, Pa."

"Somebody's gotta worry about this family."

Frank was halfway down the hill when his Uncle Fitz shouted for him to hold up. Frank reined the team to a stop, and Fitz trotted out to the wagon, his rifle over his shoulder.

"I reckoned you could use some company," Fitz said as he climbed into the seat.

"You don't have to go with me," Frank said. "This is not your responsibility."

"You're my blood, ain't you Frankie?" Fitz said and spat tobacco juice over the side. "Besides, I couldn't give you this without your pa throwin' a regular fit."

Fitz took a revolver from beneath his jacket and handed it over butt-first. Five chambers of the cylinder were loaded, capped, and greased.

"We're wastin' daylight," Fitz said. "Let's go, boy."

Frank flicked the reins.

Zachary Fenn had just finished breaking water for the stock and was on his way back to the house when Terrence Barriclaw slunk out of a hedgerow to fall into step with him.

"Trudy's been askin' about you, Zach," Terrence said. "She's been wonderin' why you and Patrick haven't been around lately. She'd like to read the cards for ye."

"She knows why we haven't come around," Zachary said, smiling. "Last time Pa found out about us being over there he wore out a strap on our backsides. I've still got the purple marks to show for it."

"Why, you're bigger than your old man," Terrence said, and cast a sideways glance. "Why didn't you just take that opportunity to teach him a thing or two. You know you could whip him."

"I'm not so sure," Zachary said, shaking his head. "I may be just as big as he is, but he knows what fightin's about. He could lick me with one hand tied behind his back, I do believe. Why, Patrick smarted off to him last week, and before you could say scat the old man had him on the ground and bleedin'. Not enough to hurt him, you understand, but enough to let old Patrick know who's boss."

"If you say so," Terrence said. "You're the one that has to take it. But that's neither here nor there. I've come on official business, and I need to speak to your pa."

"What kind of business?"

"Official business, like I said," was all Terrence would allow. Zachary walked with him up to the house, where his father was sitting at the table ciphering in his ledger book.

"How do you do, Mister Fenn," Terrence said with a bow and a wave of a dirty hand. Terrence Barriclaw was the royal messenger for the kingdom of Amarugia.

"That depends on what you want, I reckon," Francis Fenn said. "What brings you out of the hills to the Little Shannon Valley on this cold winter day? Surely nothing good, I'll wager."

"I bring greetings from King Owens."

"Greetings yourself. What does Basby Owens want?"

"Your presence has been requested at the court of justice at midnight tomorrow. Owens has a little matter he'd like to take up with you."

"How many jugs of cider am I supposed to bring?" Francis Fenn asked. The last time Owens had summoned him he had been found guilty of allowing his hogs to get away from him and roam on Amarugia ground. It had cost five crocks of hard cider to make amends.

"Oh, I wouldn't pretend to know what Owens might decide is fair," Terrence said.

"What's the charge this time?"

"You'll have to get that from Owens hisself."

"I see," Francis Fenn said. "Well, you've delivered your message. You're welcome to a cup of coffee and piece of cornbread, then it's off with you."

"Cait's cornbread?" Terrence asked. "Not the uncle's?"

"Yes, Caitlin's."

"Don't mind if I do," Terrence said and slid into a chair at the table. But his buttocks had no more than touched the seat when Caitlin was whipping him with a dishrag.

"You're filthy!" she raged. "Go wash your hands and face before you sit at this table. Go!"

Zachary laughed as Terrence made for the wash basin on the sideboard, and he winked at his sister. "I'm glad to see you treating guests like family," he teased.

It was about ten o'clock when the wagon reached the military road in Kansas Territory and Frank Fenn reined the team to a stop. It was warm, at least warmer than it had been the last few days, and the ice and snow had turned the road into beef tea and mud soup. The sun was shining down as brightly, no, brighter, than it did in summer. Frank unbuttoned his coat to let some air in.

"What do you think?" he asked.

"I don't know," Fitz said, craning his neck to see up and down the road, and then looking at the trail behind them. After leaving Missouri behind the country became flat and nearly barren of trees, except for hardwood stands along creeks and rivers. "I've had an uneasy feeling for the last few miles."

"You think we're being followed?"

"Something ain't right, but I can't lay my finger on it."

"Let's go on, then. Find a spot that has a little cover to spring old Ben out of that barrel. Here, anyone could see us for a mile either way."

Fitz nodded.

"I'm for that," he said, and spat. "Head 'em on north toward the Sante Fe trail. We'll find a good spot to do our business between here and there."

They rode on in silence, and twice the wagon became mired in mud and Frank handed the reins to his uncle, hopped down, and put his shoulder to the wheel. The third time it bogged down was on the far side of a little rise that wound down into a creek, and after ten minutes of pushing and shoving, the wagon was still stuck.

Frank took a rest and leaned against the back of the wagon, his chest heaving and sweat dripping from his chin.

"Let me help you," Fitz said, jumping down but keeping the reins in his hand. "I'll drive the team and rock this wheel up here while you push."

Frank pressed his back against the tailgate and pushed with his legs while Fitz snapped the reins and shoved against the front wheel. Frank closed his eyes and the veins in his neck stood out. There was a sucking sound as the mud lost its grip and the wagon began to move forward.

"There, that's got it," Fitz said. "Keep going."

"I think that'll be far enough."

Frank's heart sank to his stomach when he heard the voice. He opened his eyes to see the bounty hunter Jeremy Herd sitting on a horse about ten yards up the rise, a revolver in his hand. It was pointed straight at Frank's chest. Behind him was his cousin Jess, standing beside a horse, gun out.

"I don't reckon you fellas are here to help push this sorry excuse for a wagon out of this hole, are you?" Fitz felt a strange calm come over him, a response to danger that had been honed in the mountains. He knew he had to keep the Herd cousins talking, because the Hawken rifle was more than arm's reach away. Folks aren't ready to shoot you until they stop talking.

"You're crazier than a pet coon, ain't you?" Jeremy Herd asked.

"Some have allowed that," Fitz said. He transferred the reins to his other hand and asked, "Mind if I lay these down?"

"Do it slow," Jeremy Herd said. "Then we're going to settle a score over a two-hundred-dollar reward that you stole from us yesterday. Did you already take that nigger in? Or do you still have him?"

"We don't know what you're talking about," Frank said.

"Shut up," Jeremy said, shoving the revolver at him. "You're a liar."

"No need to tell tales, Frankie," Fitz said as he slowly took a step up into the wagon seat and laid the reins down. "Look here, we might as well split that reward. We got it right here, and we'll go halves with you—a hundred for each of us. What do you say? Hell, you can't blame a man for courting fortune, can you?"

Jeremy Herd didn't answer, but Fitz could hear the cylinder of the revolver lock into place as the bounty hunter thumbed the hammer back and took aim at the back of his head.

"Duck!" Frank shouted. He whipped the revolver from beneath his coat and fired in the same motion, and Herd's gun boomed a split second later. Fitz felt the slightly wild shot part the air just over his scalp.

The ball from Frank Fenn's gun struck Herd over his left breast pocket, his horse bolted, and Herd went off backward into the mud. Fitz snapped up the Hawken and brought the short barrel down to bear on Jess Herd, but stayed his trigger finger because Jess was gaping in surprise at his fallen cousin.

Jess looked up at Frank, screaming in rage, and aimed his revolver. He hadn't even got the sights in line with his eye when Fitz's rifle belched fire and smoke and a .50-caliber ball took him square in the chest.

He was dead when he hit the ground.

"Bull's-eye," Fitz said and spat tobacco juice over the side of the wagon. He drew the ramrod from beneath the barrel of the Hawken and began to reload.

"What's happening?" Ben called from inside the barrel.

"Stay in there," Frank called back.

"Your aim was off a little, Frankie," Fitz said, motioning with a jerk of his head toward Jeremy Herd. "The sonuvabitch ain't dead yet."

Revolver out, Frank waded through the mud to where the big man lay and rolled Jeremy Herd over onto his back. The bounty hunter let out a moan as his eyes came upon Frank Fenn's.

"I'll kill you," Jeremy said. He reached for his skinning knife, but was brought up short by the pain. A bloody froth covered his lips. Frank jerked the knife out of his belt and threw it out of reach.

"That varmint ain't going to kill anybody no more," Fitz said. "He's lung shot, and he's going under. You might as well put a ball between his eyes to put him out of his misery. That's how you deal with snakes, anyway."

"I can't," Frank said.

"He was going to do both of us in. We were nearly gone beavers."

"I know. But I can't."

In the end Frank thought it might have been better if he had, because it took what seemed like a long time for Herd to die, and he went hard, kicking and gurgling for air to the last.

"Are we going to leave them here like this?" Frank asked.

"I'm not going to haul their bodies back and try to explain what happened," Fitz said, climbing back into the wagon. "Are you okay, Ben?"

"Yes," came the answer from the barrel. "What happened?"

"Never you mind," Fitz said. "Come on, Frankie, let's put some ground between us and this place. There's going to be hell to pay for sure."

With desperate strength, Frank Fenn put his back to the wagon and pushed it out of the hole. Once it was rolling, Frank ran and jumped up on the seat, and Fitz kept it rolling, in the direction of Lawrence.

"I've never killed a man before," Frank said, feeling the uncomfortable pressure of the revolver in his belt.

"It gets easier," Fitz said.

They were ten miles down the trail when Frank discovered his case with the daguerreotype of Jenny was missing from his coat pocket. It lay behind them, in the mud, not far from the body of Jeremy Herd, where the dead man's brother Jake would find it three days later.

7

T HE SUN WAS LOW in the sky by the time the wagon rumbled into Lawrence. Sunlight glinted from white-washed homes and straight, New England fences, and in the center of town, in front of the brick, four-story Eldridge House—said to be the finest hotel west of the Mississippi—the Stars and Stripes flew from a tall staff. Across the street from the hotel was the county courthouse, and beside the courthouse stood a lone cannon.

The city clung to the eastern slopes of a hill that separated the valleys of the Kansas and Wakarusa rivers, and the Kansas—or Kaw, as it was more commonly called—formed the boundary between the town and the Delaware Indian Reservation to the north. Lawrence was founded in 1854 by the New England Emigrant Aid Company to be the capital of a new, slave-free state; was sacked and burned by Pro-Slavery forces in 1856; and had since been rebuilt, larger and better than before. Now, in the winter of 1859, the Wyandotte Constitution had been ratified and had won Congressional approval where a handful of earlier constitutions—both slavery and free soil—had failed. Kansas Territory was now on the verge of statehood, free statehood, but Topeka, an upstart community some thirty miles west along the Kaw River, was to be selected as the state capital. Lawrence, however, had forever won the claim as abolitionist capital of the nation.

Uncle Fitz pulled the team to a stop in front of the Eldridge House. He grinned at Frank through a tobacco-stained beard and said, "I've felt a sight more comfortable in palavering with a Crow war party for my scalp than I do right now. Which way do we go?"

"I don't know," Frank conceded, sitting suddenly straight in the seat and looking around uncomfortably. "I reckon I'd better ask somebody."

Frank jumped down from the seat, straightened his clothes, and begged the pardon of a businessman coming out of the hotel.

"Sir, could you direct me to the home of Senator Lane?"

The man removed a much-chewed cigar from the corner of his mouth and regarded Frank suspiciously.

"What business would you have with the senator?"

"We have some goods to deliver," Frank said.

"There has been much trouble with Missourians crossing the line," the man said. "You have the look of a Missourian about you."

"It is true that good Missouri dust is on my clothes," Frank replied indignantly. "But not all Missourians are ruffians, just as it is true that not all Kansans cross the line to engage in a little Jayhawking under the cover of night. I am Frank Fenn, of the Little Shannon Valley Farm in Cass County."

"Yes, I suppose so," the man said. "Lane's home is to the west, along Eighth Street. There is a shingle by the front door that proclaims it as such."

Frank rapped on the door. He heard whispers and some shuffling inside, then after a few moments a deep voice called from the other side: "Who is it?"

"Frank Fenn, sir."

"I don't know anyone by that name. Go away."

"I mean you no harm. My uncle and I have come a long way to deliver some goods that are of vital interest to you, if the newspaper accounts can be believed."

The bolt drew back and the door opened a bit. A gaunt, wild-looking man with a gray face and unkempt hair held an oil lantern in one hand and a huge Colt Walker revolver in the other. He studied Frank for a moment, paying particular attention to his hands, which rested empty at his sides.

"What kind of goods?" Lane asked, finally.

"A runaway slave, sir. My uncle and I have risked much to bring him to you."

"Where are you from?"

The revolver remained in an upright, ready position.

"From my father's farm in Cass County. I am Frank Fenn and that is my Uncle Fitz in the wagon, but I trust you will be discreet with that information, seeing as how our neighbors might not approve."

"Why are you doing this?"

"To keep him from the bounty hunters, who had nearly run him to death when we found him."

"Do you expect a reward?"

"A reward?" Frank asked. "No, sir. The only reward we expect is the easy conscience that comes from having done the right thing in the eyes of God."

The revolver barrel was lowered.

"Where's this slave?"

"In a barrel in the back of the wagon."

"Bring it in."

Frank and Uncle Fitz carried the barrel from the wagon, across the porch and into the house. Lane closed and bolted the door behind them. They placed the barrel in the middle of the room.

"Do you have something to pry with?"

Lane handed him a poker from the fireplace and Frank pried off the lid. Ben, who was sitting with his arms clutching his knees and his knees to his chest, said he was cramped so that he couldn't stand up.

Frank hooked his hands beneath his armpits and hauled him out, and Ben's eyes went wide with the sudden pain of pins and needles.

"I've done lost the feeling in both of my legs," he said, leaning on Frank for support and shaking his feet to get the circulation going again.

"Ben, this is Senator James H. Lane."

"Senator Lane," Ben said, "I am pleased to meet you, sir."

"What's wrong with his foot?" Lane asked.

"They lopped half of it off to keep me from runnin', but it didn't work," Ben said. "I ran anyway."

"Can he walk?"

"Yes sir, I walk good. Don't I, Mister Frank?"

"He can walk," Frank said.

"He'll make a soldier, then."

"A soldier?" Ben asked.

"You want to be free, don't you?" Lane asked.

"Yes, sir, I do."

"Then you're willing to fight for that freedom, aren't you?"

"I've been fightin' all my life for that. But a soldier—I never even shot a gun before."

"You will learn," Lane said. He turned to Frank. "I expect he is hungry—they always are. The poor detritus of society, washed upon our beach, with nary a morsel of food nor wrap to keep them warm. The final fruit of that peculiar institution that must be driven from the face of the earth. Go to the kitchen. My woman will fetch you a plate."

Fitz tugged at Frank's sleeve and whispered in his ear: "Let's make tracks. I get nervous when politicians start makin' speeches about God's will."

"Thank you," Ben called over his shoulder as he limped off toward the kitchen behind dour Mrs. Lane, who had sat in the shadows and not said a word during the exchange. "Tell Miss Cait good-bye for me."

"I will, Ben," Frank said. "Farewell."

Lane's smoldering eyes turned back to Frank.

"No horses or mules accompanied him to freedom?"

Frank said there were none.

"We customarily encourage slaves to liberate some of the ill-gotten gains of their masters," Lane said. "It is a practical matter, friend. It takes money to feed these souls."

"Yes, I suppose so," Frank said uncomfortably. He sat on the floor, took off his left boot, and drew a couple of bank notes from a cache hidden in the heel. Reluctantly he handed them over. Lane carefully folded the notes and slipped them into the pocket of his vest.

The wind stirred the leaves outside the window and Lane cocked his head. "Listen!" he said, reaching for the Walker which had been left on the dining table. "They are all around us, moving in the night, waiting for the unguarded moment in which to pounce. You must go."

"Yes," Frank said, "we must."

"I don't know about you," Fitz said after the door had closed behind them, "but I think the good senator is crazier than a pet coon."

. . . .

They left the team at the livery stable and put up for the night at the Eldridge House. Neither wanted to be on the road in the cold and dark, considering the trouble they had on the way to Lawrence. In the tavern down the street—technically illegal but condoned by the authorities—Fitz nursed a bottle of whiskey to calm his nerves. Frank listened for talk that the Herd cousins had been found dead, but there was none. And he dared not ask.

A man standing at the bar held a copy of the Leavenworth paper toward the lamplight and was reading aloud a story about presidential candidate Abraham Lincoln, of Illinois, addressing a crowd from the steps of the Planters Hotel in Leavenworth.

"It was the largest mass meeting ever held on Kansas soil," the man read. "When questioned about the hanging of John Brown, Mr. Lincoln asserted that the attack on Harpers Ferry was wrong for two reasons: the first, that it was a violation of law, and the second, that it was futile. He went on to say that every citizen has a peaceful means of expression in regard to slavery, that of the ballot box."

Frank was thinking of another trail to take back home to Cass County—a trail which would avoid the bloody mudhole where the bounty hunters had met their end—when the door of the saloon flew open. A figure wrapped in buffalo robes stepped inside and stamped his boots upon the plank floor.

"Damn, but it is colder than a well-digger's butt," he roared. "You had better pour something with some fire in it to warm this child up."

The layers of buffalo robes came off to reveal a man of stout build, in his middle thirties, with red hair that flowed to his shoulders. He grabbed the drink and not so much drank it as threw it down his throat, smacking the glass back on the bar and indicating another. When he had downed the second, and a third, he wiped the back of his hand across his mouth and allowed that they had better send for the sheriff.

"What for?" the bartender demanded. "You feel like starting some trouble tonight, Babe?"

"The trouble has already been started and finished, but not by me," the man said. "The Herd cousins are lying dead in the mud a piece down the old Sante Fe trail."

. . . .

To Frank's consternation the loud man with the red hair came and sat down at their table while he waited for the sheriff to arrive. The man looked at Frank, and then Uncle Fitz, then stuck out a rough hand.

"They call me Babe Hudspeth," he said. "I came to Kansas Territory in 1858 from Ohio and was foolish enough to undertake a gold expedition to Pikes Peak, from which I gained not one cent but nearly lost my life. We were caught in the mountains by a fierce blizzard, my companions froze to death, and I was obliged to eat them to stay alive. My friend George Cordell was especially tasty, but his missus was even finer."

Frank looked at him in horror, but Fitz shook his head and poured Hudspeth a drink.

"I'd say you've spent some time in the mountains, but it weren't on no pilgrim trail," Fitz said. "A liar like you must have been a free trapper."

"I knew by your clothes you was a child of the mountains," Hudspeth said. "We have to stick together, since there ain't no life in the mountains left, not for a free trapper. Damn, but it is good to see a friendly face. These New England types have absolutely no sense of humor. I'll bet I've told that story about eating old George and his wife a dozen times, and this is the first time anybody has so much as cracked a smile."

"So there was some trouble on the Clinton Road?" Fitz asked.

"There was," Hudspeth said. "But I can't say I'm going to shed any tears for the Herd cousins. They done the same to others lots of times, and it just seems fair that somebody paid them back."

"Any idea who done it?" Fitz asked.

"Could have been anybody," Hudspeth said. "From the looks of the carcasses, I'd say it was somebody packin' a Navy colt and a big bore rifle, maybe a Sharps. Old Jake Herd will be mad as hell when he finds out."

"Jake Herd?" Frank asked.

"Jeremy's brother," Hudspeth said. "Jake is the biggest, meanest sonuvabitch on the border. He and his fellows hang out on the sandbar just across the river, on the Delaware Reservation side. Jake makes his living by stealing slaves in Missouri and then selling them back to their owners. Compared to Jake, the rest of those boys on the sandbar are children."

8

FRANCIS FENN stood in the circle of light cast by the torches on either side of Basby Owens' rough-hewn throne. Saturday night "court" was the mainstay entertainment for the score of residents of the backwoods kingdom of Amarugia, and most of them lounged in the darkness beyond the torchlight, pulling their wraps tight against the cold and speculating on the case to be tried. Somewhere in the winter night an owl hooted, and from deeper in the woods another answered.

Owens sprawled in the rough, split-wood chair, one large hand wrapped lovingly around a jug of hard cider, the other gripping the carved bone handle of a walking stick. The carving depicted a dragon in a carnal embrace with a maiden in such a way that the girl's ample buttocks nested in the palm of Owens' hand. Owens regarded the walking stick as his scepter, a symbol of the magic and superstition with which he ruled his tiny kingdom. He never spoke of where the walking stick came from, but he often allowed that the carving represented the moment of his conception.

Any man was free to challenge his rule by attempting to wrestle the scepter away from Owens, but few were foolish enough to have actually tried. Owens towered over most men—he was six foot two and weighed two hundred fifty pounds—and his favorite method for dispatching opponents was to snap their backs across his knee. Even if he couldn't whip you with his fists, he was likely to carve you up with the eight-inch blade concealed in the handle of the walking stick. The last challenger, a strapping Jackson County lad who had disputed Owens for the right to court an

Amarugia girl, had died on his knees with his guts poured out on the dirt before him.

Francis Fenn knew Basby Owens was a dangerous man, and he did not relish his visits to the backwoods court held inside a ring of shacks along Owens Creek. But the eldest Fenn also understood that Owens respected courage and strength, and he was determined never to come before him with bended knee or bowed head. To do so would be an invitation for the petty tyrant to run roughshod over operations of the family farm. So he stood with his legs firmly planted in the soft red dirt while he waited for Owens to speak.

"Fenn," Owens said, at length, "you're getting old. There's snow in your hair and a caution to your walk. You're not the lad we once knew. It's not wise for someone who has grown so long in the tooth to be trifling with the laws of the land."

"When I need your advice, I'll ask it," Francis said. "I was through with kings when I left Ireland twenty-three years ago, and I'll be damned if I will ever bend a knee again. I'm here only because I respect my neighbors, no matter how crazy they are, and I don't mind sharing a few jugs of cider now and again."

"I'm afraid cider will not make amends for this offense," Owens said, and pointed the walking stick at Terrence Barriclaw. "Read the charges."

Terrence unrolled a sheet of paper and cleared his throat.

"The accused, Francis Fenn, Master of the Little Shannon Valley Farm, is charged with threatening the well-being of the subjects of Good King Owens by bringing stock of uncertain origin into the Kingdom of Amarugia," Terrence read. "This is an especially serious offense, considering the scourge upon livestock that has visited the border counties in recent years in the form of Trail Fever."

"What say you to the charge?" Owens asked.

"The charge is preposterous," Francis said. "These cattle have been wintered in the Cherokee Neutral Lands. If anyone has a warrant to be cautious, it's me—I lost forty head last year alone to the Texas Fever. But fear is not going to prevent me from rebuilding my stock. Not all cattle are diseased."

"But there's no way to tell, is there?"

"Not unless they start dropping, and if they do, I will shoot them myself and bury the carcasses rather than pass the fever along to the rest of the county."

"It may be too late for that," Owens said. "These cows have already been grazing loose along the river, in which case none of your herd may be safe—and none of ours, either."

Francis swallowed hard. Owens was right enough about the stock getting away from Patrick, but that didn't necessarily mean an epidemic. It was too early to tell if the cattle carried the fever or not, or if they had picked it up along the trail home.

"I have no reason to believe this stock carries the fever," Francis said, "and neither do you. Your fear is getting the best of you, Owens. You are the one who is acting like an old man."

Owens stirred on his throne. The jug of cider fell to the ground as he leaned forward on his walking stick and regarded Francis Fenn from beneath tangled brows.

The crowd caught its breath.

Terrence Barriclaw took a few steps back.

"The last pup that called me old was broken over my knee," Owens said.

"So I am a pup, now?" Francis asked, laughing. "It seems your age has affected your mind as well. Don't worry, I'm not wanting to take your cane away from you. But I'll be damned if I will put up with this foolishness for one minute longer."

Owens felt the eyes of the crowd upon him and his cheeks flushed redder than usual. He looked beyond the firelight at the expectant huddled shapes, then back at Fenn.

"Such talk can get a man banished from these parts," Owens said.

"Such a sentence would be a blessing," Fenn said. "Let us put aside the trimmings and get to the meat of the matter, Owens. Speak plainly. What is it that you want from me?"

"A tax upon your stock," Owens said.

"By God, you do act like a king. What manner of tax?"

"That's no easy matter," Owens said, stroking his tangled beard. "But I believe something on the order of, say, eight bits for every head of foreign stock would do nicely."

"Not only a king, but a pirate as well," Fenn said. "I will not pay fifty cents, much less a dollar, cash money, for the privilege of owning my own cows. Two bits is the best I can offer."

Owens shook his head.

"You are taking a terrible risk, Fenn," he said.

"The only thing at risk here is your pride," Francis said. "Look here, is there no way we can settle this? Bring up that stump, there. We will arm wrestle for this tax. If you win, I will pay your dollar. But if I win, you must accept twenty-five cents, and also agree to protect my herd from some of your hunters who have difficulty distinguishing a deer from a cow."

"And what if these foreign cows are diseased?"

"Then you must help me destroy the herd to keep the fever from spreading. Agreed?"

"Agreed," Owens said, laying his stick aside and shedding his shirt and coat. "Bring up the stump," he bellowed. "By God, I will make short work of this one."

Terrence Barriclaw rolled the chopping stump out into the center of the firelight, and two stools were produced for the men to sit upon. Francis took off his coat, folded it, and laid it aside. Then he rolled his sleeves up over his elbows and sat down across from Owens.

Basby Owens grinned as he flexed his massive shoulders and shifted his weight on the stool to find a comfortable spot. Francis studied the surface of the chopping stump and found a place where his elbow could find suitable purchase. When they clasped hands, his hand was nearly lost in Owens' huge paw. The crowd drew close as Terrence tied their hands together with a piece of rawhide.

"On the count of three," Owens said, and nodded to Terrence.

"One," Terrence said.

The paw began to squeeze like a vise around Francis' hand.

"Two."

The muscles in Owens' arm began to gather.

"Three!"

Francis felt as if his arm were being wrenched out of his socket. Owens bared his teeth and the veins in his forehead and his neck stood out like cords. Francis' hand wavered and he lost a few inches. Then he sucked in his breath and began to let it out in a measured, controlled way. His hand was still trembling, but he had stalled Owens' advance.

Francis focused on a spot on the bridge of Owens' nose and concentrated on breathing. He imagined his hand was made of stone, his arm of oak.

The bones in their arms popped and groaned, but after thirty seconds the hands remained upright.

Owens was still holding his breath. Sweat began to bead on Owens' forehead, then rolled down to sting his eyes. His lungs burned and his face turned an even deeper shade of red. His hand began to tremble. This angered him and he strained even harder.

At forty-five seconds it felt as if the bones in Francis' hand were being crushed in some enormous, malevolent vise, and he forced himself to repeat: *stone doesn't feel.*

Owens' face was now purple and he feared the top of his head was going to blow right off. At just over the one minute mark he let out his breath in a great, foul-smelling gust. His hand faltered and Francis made the best of it, driving Owens' hand down to a 45-degree angle.

Owens sucked in wind and recovered somewhat, bringing his hand back to nearly the upright position. But he could not recover his breath, despite his panting, and fatigue washed over him. The knowledge that he was spent settled in his stomach like a cold stone. It frightened him. He had never lost a fight, but none of his fights had ever lasted over thirty seconds. Not only did he not have the wind for longer, he never suspected he would ever need it. Still, he could not simply give up, and for another twenty seconds—which seemed like twenty minutes—he struggled.

When Francis finally felt the strength begin to drain from Owens he did not drive for a finish, but kept up the steady, relentless pressure, pragmatically folding Owens' arm down toward the surface of the stump. Owens gave the last three inches and Francis rapped his knuckles into the stump.

Owens howled in pain, as a child might, but the pain was from knowing the bitter taste of defeat rather than having his knuckles bloodied.

Francis did not gloat over his victory. His head was swimming but he managed to stand, unroll his sleeves, and call for his coat. Francis knew Owens was a dangerous man, but of necessity he was a man of his word. Owens would not disgrace himself further by backing out on a public deal.

"Thank you for the sport," Francis said as he laid seven dollars and fifty cents in coin on the stump. "A word of advice on your next contest: don't hold your breath."

Owens remained on the stool. The sweat shone from his naked upper body, and he was still huffing like a locomotive. He cast an eye upward at Francis.

"You Fenns are not as slight as you appear to be," Owens said.

"We seldom are," Francis Fenn said.

Patrick Fenn had snuck out of an upstairs window after the others thought he was asleep, and he had watched from the safety of the crowd while his father had arm-wrestled Basby Owens. Now he slunk back in the shadows while his father strode past, lest he get the whipping of his life. As he stepped backward he fell into the arms of Trudy Barriclaw, who in turn had been watching Patrick.

Trudy began to speak but Patrick held a finger to his lips to shush her. Trudy grabbed his finger and kissed it, then drew his hand along her cheek.

"I've missed you," she said.

"Quiet," Patrick hissed.

Trudy had dark hair and liquid brown eyes. The coffee-colored skin of her childlike face seemed to be perpetually smudged with camp smoke. She wore a dirty white blouse and a flowing purple skirt that was cinched at the waist by a wide leather belt. Tucked inside the belt was a crude trade knife that she used to clean game and eat with and to discourage advances. It was a shame, she thought as she stood holding Patrick's hand against her cheek, that she hadn't the sand to use it to encourage advances as well. Even though their fumbling attempts at lovemaking in the last few weeks had ended, well, prematurely, she ached at the thought of him lying against her skin.

Trudy was two years younger than Patrick and they had known each other since they were young children, when their common interests were wading in the creeks and collecting bird nests and whatever else they could find along the deer runs and rabbit traces near their homes. Trudy's mother was a mixed blood, the result of a temporary union between a French trapper and an Osage squaw, and her last name was an Indian corruption of the trapper's name. Her mother was an exceptional woman who could read and write French and call the Indian signs, but her particular gift was as a prophetess. She died the year of the Great

Comet, 1858, and on her deathbed she told Trudy that a time of great tribulation was coming for the whites. The only material things she had left Trudy were a trunk of old-fashioned trade clothes and a much-used deck of Tarot cards that had been printed the year that Napoleon had died on St. Helena.

"Come back to the shack with me," Trudy said when she was sure Patrick's father had gone. "I want to read your fortune."

She started off with his hand in hers. Patrick allowed himself to be led down the path to her shack, where she placed him on the floor and lit candles and had him shuffle the cards three times. She took the deck and laid the cards in a pattern before him.

She gave a start when she had laid the last card down.

"Something has changed," she said.

"We can do this later," Patrick said impatiently, and ran his hand down the inside of her blouse.

"No," she said, slapping his hand away, although she did not feel much like resisting. "This first. This is important. Things have changed since the last time I read your cards. Look, there are new faces: the Lovers, the Tower, the Hanged Man. I don't understand."

She trembled inside. She did understand, and she did not like it. The cards spelled calamity and despair for the pair of lovers, and she feared what it meant for her and Patrick. She tried to concentrate on the cards, tried to focus her mind, but her fear kept clouding her judgment. Finally she swept the pattern away with a wave of her hand, hopelessly jumbling the cards.

"Why'd you do that?" Patrick asked. "I thought you said it was important."

"I was wrong," Trudy said. She grabbed him by the lapels and pulled him down on top of her. She kissed him long and deep, and while she kissed him she shoved his coat down over his shoulders, and unbuttoned his shirt. Frustrated a moment by his long underwear she finally succeeded in pulling all his layers of clothes free and snaking out of her own. Their union was just as urgent but somewhat less awkward this time, and afterward she rested her head against his bare chest and listened to him breathe.

Zachary were solid enough, but Patrick was too much like Uncle Fitz—living only for the day. What had gone wrong, and what could he do to keep Patrick from disgracing himself and the family? The land, perhaps, would tame him. Being rooted, having a sense of stewardship, making an honest living from honest labor and the beneficent earth, could redeem a soul.

The land would be his legacy. He had carved a home out of what was wilderness less than a generation earlier, and that anchor would last for many generations hence. He imagined a time when children would again play in the shadow of the big, ramshackle house, and he smiled.

His stride faltered. He stopped and knelt on one knee, striving to catch his breath. He glanced upward at the stars blinking in the night sky, the new moon sailing in her course, and the chimney smoke from the house that seemed to float among them. He couldn't remember a time when the farm looked so beautiful, so full of promise.

Pain spread from the center of his chest into both arms now, and up into his throat. His ears rang and his vision narrowed to the tiny patch of ground where he knelt. Francis Fenn fumbled with the buttons of his collar trying to relieve the pressure. It felt as if his chest were being crushed in the coils of some huge snake.

He rolled over onto his back, his arms doubled over his chest, his boot heels digging furrows into the ground. He tried to call out, but could do no more than gasp for breath. He felt the world slipping away, but he was no longer afraid. He was held up, comforted, embraced by the feel of the land against his back. Soon he would be folded into it, tucked beside Mary beneath the big oak on that lonely hillside that would be lonely no more.

Soon he would be home.

9

HIS ARMS AND LEGS leaden, Francis Fenn trudged across the barren fields toward the house, where a telltale lamp in the kitchen window showed that Caitlin was waiting up for him. He would have to strap Patrick for slipping out to visit that Indian trash, Trudy Barriclaw—he had seen them, of course, together in the shadows—but that would have to wait until morning. He was too tired to chase Patrick through the woods tonight. He was more tired, in fact, than he had ever remembered.

Owens had been right. He was getting old. Had he really needed to beat Owens at his own game, or had he succumbed to his own vanity? His arm, and especially his hand, ached with the memory of Owens' grip. He could scarcely make a fist with his right hand, and he was afraid that some of the bones might be broken. It would take a long time to heal.

He had come to be afraid of a great many things these days: drought, grasshoppers, trail fever, his neighbors along the border. He worried about how Frank and his Uncle Fitz were faring across the line in Kansas Territory, and whether there would be any more trouble over runaway slaves. He worried that his time to be in the ground would come before his boys had learned how to live and manage the farm. He worried about Caitlin and whether her devotion to the family would make her a spinster. In another year or two she would be past the age when most girls were married. Yet he couldn't imagine how the farm would get along without her.

He was especially concerned for Patrick, who seemed completely devoid of a sense of humility or responsibility. Frank and

10

JENNY LOWELL came to the Little Shannon Valley three weeks from the day that Francis Fenn was buried in the hillside plot. Frank had brooded over the uncertainty of life for a week after the funeral, turning things over a thousand times in his mind, walking the floor at night, starting a dozen letters and tearing them up. Finally he simply wrote: "I love you. Life is short. Let us not delay." She understood.

She took the train from Boston to its terminus at St. Joseph, where she boarded a steamboat on the Missouri River. Frank met the boat at Westport Landing, loaded her bags and trunks into the wagon, and wrapped his bride in a buffalo robe against the fierce winter wind. They drove straight to Harrisonville, where they were married, and he deposited her upon the doorstep of her new home two days later.

She was unprepared for what she found.

Rough-looking men were shooting all of the stock on the farm and dragging the carcasses behind a team of oxen to a ravine that would serve as a mass grave. The roughest-looking one of the bunch, a veritable giant with a tangle of hair and beard, was supervising the others. As the wagon passed the giant doffed his hat and gave her a courtly bow.

All of it frightened her.

"I'm sorry," Frank said. "I meant to tell you about this. The cattle were infected with Spanish fever. This is necessary to save the rest of the stock in the county."

Frank left her on the doorstep as he took the wagon around back to put up the team. The house, of rough-hewn log and native stone, was as wild-looking as the rest of the country she had seen. She warily regarded the crossed elk horns above the door. She did not know whether to knock, or to go on in, or to wait for Frank. Finally she managed to rap lightly on the door, and when there was no response, she tried the door and found that it swung free on its hinges.

"Hello?" she asked, closing the door behind her and creeping in.

It was dark inside. A pot simmered over a low fire in the fireplace. A basket of mending sat near the hearth, where the light was best, but the needles had been deserted. In the far corner, sitting in her father's rocking chair, sat Caitlin Fenn. Her hands gripped the arms of the chair and her feet rested on the floor.

"You must be Jenny," Caitlin said, but did not rise.

"Yes," Jenny said. "I am pleased to meet you—I have heard so much about you and the farm and the boys—"

"Yes, the boys," Caitlin said. "The boys. Well. Frank has decided that you and him are going to share father's room. It's to the left, just around the corner. Biggest bedroom in the house."

"Thank you," Jenny said, and walked toward the bedroom. She stopped at the corner and turned. "Caitlin," she said, "are you feeling ill? You look so forlorn sitting there."

"Don't worry about me," Caitlin said, not bothering to look at Jenny. "I'm fine. Things will just take a little getting used to. Can you cook?"

"A little," Jenny said uncertainly.

"Can you dress game? Squirrels? Rabbits? Can you clean fish? Can you make soap or tend to sick animals or stitch up the boys' wounds when they hurt themselves or stay up all night with them when they have the fever?"

"I'm sure I can't do any of those things nearly as well as you can," Jenny said softly. "I couldn't replace you, not even if I wanted to. Sometimes I fret that I'll never be able to take as good care of Frank as you can, and I used to worry that he would never love me as much as he loves you. You ought to see the look he gets in his eyes when he talks about his little sister and how good and kind and what a comfort she is. But I can help, if you'll let me. Please, let me. I want us to be friends."

Caitlin's lower lip was trembling.

"It's been awful with Papa gone," she said. Tears began rolling down her cheeks. She hadn't cried once, not at the funeral or after. "I miss him so much. When I was little he used to rock me in this chair and sing me songs. Now he's gone forever and things are so terrible here at the farm and I don't think I'll ever be able to smile again."

Jenny went to her, knelt beside the chair, and pulled Caitlin to her. Caitlin resisted at first, then relented and flung her arms around Jenny's neck.

"I've been so afraid of letting the boys know how I feel," Caitlin cried. "I was afraid that if I crumbled the rest of them would, too. Papa was so important to us. He *was* the farm. And then when Frank said he was going to marry you and bring you here, I was afraid they wouldn't need me anymore. That you would do everything better than I could, that you would be smarter and prettier and kinder. And you are."

"Nonsense," Jenny said, smoothing Caitlin's hair.

"But you must be or Frank wouldn't have fallen in love with you," she said. "He's always talking about you and what books you've shared and the kind of music you enjoy and what you think about politics."

"You're important to Frank, too."

Caitlin looked up at her for the first time. Her eyes were red with crying and her face was blotchy.

"You don't understand," she said. "There was so much to be done here, and Papa didn't think it was important for girls to go to school. He loved me, but he didn't think it was important."

"What do you mean, dear?"

"I can't even *read*."

11

March 1860

LIFE BECAME increasingly difficult on the farm as the new year of 1860 unfolded: the previous year's drought continued unabated, the grasshoppers returned, the crops failed. Hunger was common. Across the line in Kansas Territory, thirty thousand settlers threw down their hoes in disgust and returned East. But the Fenns, blessed with their valley along the South Fork of the Grand River, persisted, and they shared their larder with any of their neighbors that might need it.

Fitz used his rifle to keep meat on the table while the boys worked from sunup to sundown tending the crops. Caitlin taught Jenny to shuck corn and to cook and to use walnuts to dye the boys' homespun clothing. In the mornings when everyone else was gone they would rest from the chores for fifteen or twenty minutes, and Jenny would use an old slate on which to teach Caitlin her letters. Imagine, Caitlin often said, being able to read the Bible for one's self.

The old days of prosperity were gone, when they could rely on the stock to see them through, and Frank was bitterly disappointed that he could not share his past affluence—the affluence that had enabled Pa to send him back East to school—with his new wife. Patrick's visits to Trudy Barriclaw's shack became less and less frequent, partly because he was just too tired and partly because it reminded him of the night his pa had died.

Zachary made the trek to Trading Post as often as he could, and each time he brought along a story for Sarah, more often than not culled from the trunk of books that had accompanied Jenny. Some were the romances of Sir Walter Scott, others were the plays of Shakespeare, but Sarah's favorites were always the poems, poems of any kind. Zachary loved Sarah, and knew they should be married, but he had no illusions about the ability of the farm to support one more family. Besides, there were two brothers ahead of him to lay claim to the land.

So on the way to Trading Post he often made detours to look for a piece of land to homestead one day, and in the first weekend of November he found it. Situated along Sugar Creek was the most pleasant patch of earth he thought he had ever seen. The bottom-land was dark and rich, and still green with grass, and there was a shady spot on the side of a wooded hill where he pictured the cabin.

Riding together on Raven he brought Sarah to the place, and she laughed and clapped her hands and described how everything would be, including where the children would sleep. He had not asked her to marry him, but she already knew how he felt. He promised that as soon as the Little Shannon Valley Farm was on its own, and no longer so sorely in need of his back, they would return and make a home.

They sat together on the grassy hillside, with Sarah's arm laced around his, and he read from a new book that he had found in the bountiful trunk. It contained many strange and wonderful tales, and Sarah immediately declared her new favorite a poem called, "Annabel Lee."

"Will you love me like that when I'm dead and gone?" she teased.

"I will love you like that always," Zachary said, and kissed her hand.

Then it began to rain, and the rain began to freeze, and the ice began to coat the trees and lie like a sheet on the ground. Zachary threw his India-rubber slicker around Sarah and, holding her tight in front of him, guided sure-footed Raven through the beauty of the ice-laden land toward home.

The schoolmaster, William Clarke Quantrill, left Stanton at the end of the spring term and drifted up to Lawrence. He was twenty-three and his melancholy deepened. He was ill much of the time, he could not bring himself to look for steady work, and

he brooded over which direction might bring him the respect he
so desperately wanted. He spent most of his time with the friends
he had made among the Delaware Indians, or with the ruffians
that milled about on the sandbars along the Kaw. He was quiet
and secretive, and he adopted the name Charley Hart as if to shed
his former self and become more like the rough men, the men of
action, that he admired. He was skilled at taking on the color of
whichever group of people he found himself among, whether it
was the pro-slavery ruffians or the fanatical Redlegs. He never
bragged but often dropped hints that he was more important
than he appeared to be; with a conspiratorial wink he would discourage questions about his real name by suggesting he was a
federal Indian agent conducting some type of intrigue. At other
times he played the abolitionist or the loyal Southerner. In a time
when such foolishness would get other men killed, Quantrill's
posturing was so convincing it seemed that any contradictions his
associates heard were just further proof of the young man's brilliant schemes to deceive the enemy.

When he was on the south side of the river he hung about
Nathan Stone's City Hotel and Stone's pretty daughter Lydia, but
any question of a serious relationship seemed always out of reach.
Charley Hart worshiped Lydia and showered her with compliments and gifts, but he allowed that his destiny was too important
to be trifled with by getting married and living as other folks.

He wrote another letter to his mother, in which he expressed
outrage that the money he had sent her had been lost in the mails.
He complained about his lack of direction, his general dissatisfac-
tion with life, and his longing for the carefree life of childhood.
He wanted a home and family of his own. He said he was nearly
through with Kansas, and he suggested that he would be coming
back to Ohio sometime soon.

But he never did.

It was his last letter to her, although she lived for many more
years. Quantrill's poetic streak, which was always to the fore when
he was addressing women, ran strong in that last letter.

Quantrill wrote:

> It seems that man is doomed to aspire after happiness but never in
> reality attain it, for God intended that this earth should be the earth,
> and not a heaven for mortal man.

12

April 1861

THE RAIN beat upon the roof and lashed at the windows and the wind made the front door tremble. The worst of the storm was on the dark horizon, where lightning split the sky and thunder shook the earth. Although it was still early in the afternoon, the weather had driven the Fenns to abandon their toil and seek the shelter of the house. The rest was a welcome break from the daily monotony of the fields.

Inside the great room the fire blazed brightly and Frank Fenn sat in a chair near the hearth. He had shed his soaking boots and socks, and his bare feet were resting on the warm stones. In his hand was a mug of strong coffee, and sitting on the floor by his side, Jenny was quilting. But her mind didn't seem to be on her work and she often pricked her finger with the needle. At times she sat with the work ignored in her lap while she gazed at Frank, looking as if she were trying to find the proper words to speak of something important.

Uncle Fitz was smoking his pipe and taking his leisure in a chair in the corner, thinking of all the storms he had ridden out in the mountains. They all had been beautiful, but on this afternoon his joints at least were thankful for the roof overhead. The fire was a comfort and soon his jaw went slack and he was dozing.

Caitlin sat in the rocker with the family Bible open on her lap. Every so often her brow would knit and she would spell a word for Jenny and ask her how to pronounce it, and even though the brothers would chorus an answer, Caitlin would listen only to

Jenny. None of them had ever offered to teach her how to read, she said, and she wasn't going to let them help her now.

Zachary was stretched out on the floor, using his coat for a pillow, feeling the approaching thunder worry the foundations of the house. He was thinking about Sarah, and wondering how long it would take to build a cabin on the land near Sugar Creek. He reckoned it wouldn't take more than a week or two, with his brothers helping, for a one-room cabin with a loft. A man named Smith owned the claim and wanted ninety-five dollars for it, and Zachary hoped to gain the permission of his older brother and begin homesteading sometime that spring. He felt that he had waited long enough. Frank seemed to be in a good humor, and he resolved to speak his mind on it before the day was out.

Patrick was sitting on a stool nearby, using a stone to sharpen his belt knife. There were a dozen cutting chores a day on the farm, and while it was true that a dull knife was more dangerous than a sharp one, Patrick's attachment to the knife went beyond utility. He had found the blade in the mud down by Owens Creek one day. It was an old-fashioned knife like the kind the trappers carried, and the handles had rotted away, but it was of good steel. Patrick had fashioned walnut handles for it and secured them with brass rivets and he had polished the steel until it shone again. When finished, he found the knife had good balance and he would often pause in his chores to practice throwing it at a fence post or tree trunk. In time, he could put the knife in the center of a playing card at twenty paces. But Patrick's attention to the knife made Jenny uncomfortable and she finally asked him to put it away.

"I'm not going to stick anybody," Patrick protested. He was testing the blade by shaving the hairs from his forearm.

"No, but I'm afraid you're going to cut *yourself*," she said. "The tension of waiting for you to bleed is making me quite ill, so please do as I say."

Frank nodded.

Patrick put the knife back in its sheath on his belt and put the stone in his pocket. He added another log to the fire and sullenly watched it burn.

"I'm sorry, Patrick," Jenny said, and laid the quilt aside. "I have had something on my mind that is causing me to be so cross. I hope you will forgive me."

Patrick softened.

"There's nothing to forgive," he said. "I was making a nuisance of myself."

"What's wrong, dear?" Frank asked. "Are you ill?"

"No, nothing like that," Jenny said and smiled. She had eagerly read the papers for news since the first of the Southern states began to secede, sure that the war to end slavery had finally come. War was a terrible thing, but she and Frank both felt it might be necessary to purge the country of the evil of slavery. Now it appeared that a fight would be necessary to preserve the Union as well, even in their own backyard. Even though Missourians had voted overwhelmingly the previous November to preserve the Union and peacefully settle the slavery question, Governor Claiborne Jackson—a leader of the state's small but vocal group of secessionists—had called the General Assembly into special session and ordered the pro-slavery State Guard into summer encampments.

Frank had written to the military command at St. Louis offering his services, and in the weeks spent waiting for a reply Jenny's resolve had softened somewhat. Now that the Confederates had fired on Fort Sumter and President Lincoln had called for seventy-five thousand men for a real shooting war, she was not so sure that she wanted Frank to accept a commission with the Union army.

"I'm afraid," she told Frank. "I don't want you to leave."

"But I thought we were of one mind," Frank said. "I believe it is my duty to God and to my country. My father enlisted when the country called upon him for the War with Mexico, and I can do no less. The farm is doing middling well and all the papers say the fight won't last but a few weeks. Surely I'll be home in time for harvest."

The storm raged outside. Lightning struck the oak on the hillside where their parents were buried, splitting the tree and sending its massive branches crashing to the ground in a shower of sparks, and the house shook with the concussion. Caitlin closed her Bible and laid it aside.

"Patrick, Zachary," she said. "Come with me to make sure that the windows and doors in the back of the house are secure. It is blowing something fierce."

"You don't need both of us to—"

"I asked for you to help me," Caitlin said sternly.

"Come on," Zachary said, getting to his knees. "She means for us to clear out so that Frank and Jenny can chew this thing a little finer. Frank knows damn well how I feel."

Zachary reckoned the time was not good to be asking Frank's permission to begin homesteading on the Big Sugar. He slapped Uncle Fitz's knee on his way past to wake him up.

"What?" Fitz asked.

"Come on," Zachary said, and inclined his head toward the couple. "They need some space."

"Oh. I reckon I better see to it that we have enough dry kindling to fix supper," Fitz said, struggling out of the chair to follow Patrick into the kitchen.

"Jenny," Frank said when they were finally alone. "What is it? What has frightened you so? Are you afraid I'm going to get myself killed?"

"You know I'll always worry about that," she said.

"You know I'll be careful," he said.

"Yes, I know."

Jenny let her head sink to her chest. Firelight painted her face, reflecting from her high cheekbones and broad forehead. Frank placed a hand under her chin and turned her face toward his.

"I know I am acting foolishly," she said. "Why, just consider all the women who have gone through this before me."

"That's right," Frank said. "Women have been sending their men off to war for thousands of years."

"No, that's not what I meant," Jenny said, and her lips trembled. She grasped his hand and held it tightly.

"Frank," she said, "I'm with your child."

Frank whooped with joy and his outburst brought the others back into the great room. Frank had come out of the chair and swept Jenny up in his arms and was holding her above him in delight. She felt as light as a bird in his arms. The others stood and stared from the doorway and when Frank realized Jenny's feet were dangling above the floor he gently placed her in the chair and kissed her forehead.

"We're going to have a baby," Frank explained.

Zachary and Patrick shook Frank's hand and slapped him on the back and looked at Jenny in wonder. Fitz went to fetch the jug of cider, and as he passed out of the room he remarked—just loud enough for the others to hear—that Frank was such a lamebrain he was surprised the boy had managed it without help.

Caitlin put her arms around Jenny's neck and hugged her tightly, then retrieved the Bible from beside the chair in the corner. She opened it to the passage she had been studying earlier.

"I want to read something," Caitlin said, her voice shaking a bit. She had not read aloud to anyone but Jenny. "This is from the Gospel according to Luke, Chapter One, starting at Verse Twenty-Eight: 'And the angel came in unto her, and said, "Hail, thou that art highly favored, the Lord is with thee; blessed art thou among women." And when she saw him she was troubled at his saying, and cast in her mind what manner of salutation this should be. And the angel said unto her, "Fear not, Mary: for thou hast found favor unto God. And, behold, thou shalt conceive in thy womb, and bring forth a son, and shalt call his name Jesus." ' "

"That was beautiful, Cait," Jenny said. "Thank you."

"I'm going to write the baby's name in the front," Caitlin said, her hand caressing the cover, "just like Papa did for each one of us."

Fitz returned with the jug and some tin cups and he poured himself and the boys a round. He poured an extra cup and set it on the mantel.

"Who's that one for?" Patrick asked.

"That one's for your father, boys," Fitz said, and lifted his own cup high. "Here's to Frank and Jenny's baby—and to all the babies that will come—here's to a new generation of Fenns. May they stride the earth like giants, may they have the courage of their fathers and the grace of their mothers, and may they never forget where they come from."

The rain was pouring down Jake Herd's neck and back as he walked his horse into the livery stable at Independence. Herd had planned to snatch three slaves from a man named Burroughs that lived on the outskirts of town, but taut nerves and anxiety along the border were interfering with his business. A local patrol had come by and grilled Herd and his two companions about why they were lurking on the road at night. They had no reasonable explanation and were forced to move on. Even the weather seemed to be against Herd tonight; he decided to seek shelter, buy a bottle of whiskey, and get stinking drunk.

The neighborhood patrols had increased since the fight at the Morgan Walker farm had heightened fears about slave-stealing abolitionists sneaking across the line. Last December, Bill Quantrill had conspired with a group of five Quakers to free the twenty-six slaves belonging to Walker, who was a wealthy planter. Quantrill volunteered to reconnoiter the farm for his five Lawrence comrades, but instead he rode directly to the front door of the Walker home and warned the family of the plot. When the Quakers returned after dark, the Walker family was waiting on the porch with loaded shotguns.

One of the Quakers was killed on the spot, two others made a clean escape, and two wounded men who had hid themselves in the woods were hunted down and killed by Quantrill and his new friends, the Walkers. Quantrill became a local celebrity and began organizing militia forces to guard the neighborhoods from abolitionists.

Quantrill told a long story about how he had come to Kansas Territory to join his only brother in an expedition to Pikes Peak. Montgomery's raiders—or Lane's, as Quantrill sometimes told the story—had swept down on them one night while they camped at the Little Cottonwood River. The Jayhawkers robbed them, killed his brother, and left Quantrill seriously wounded. He spent three days lingering near death guarding the body of his brother. An old Shawnee Indian ventured by, buried the brother, and nursed Quantrill back to health. Quantrill allowed that he had then taken an assumed name—Charley Hart—and had slowly and carefully infiltrated the Jayhawkers in order to plot his revenge. One by one he had secretly killed those responsible for his brother's death —the two killed during the Walker raid was nearly the last of them.

There were those that believed Quantrill's story, and others who were suspicious but found it a convenient explanation for the ambush of the Quakers. The story was widely repeated and taken as irrefutable evidence of the treachery of the abolitionists. Herd, who came to know Quantrill during his time in Lawrence, knew the story to be entirely false but grinned every time he thought of Bill Quantrill sitting back in a chair at someone's dinner table and unwinding the whopper. Bill's talent lay in telling folks what they wanted to believe.

Herd gave his horse to the boy inside the livery stable, then walked next door to the dreary little saloon. He shook the rain from his clothes and warmed his hands over the stove and bought a bottle of whiskey.

He pulled a leather case from his pocket, opened it, and laid it on the counter. He uncorked the bottle and took a long pull as the owner of the saloon regarded the daguerreotype of the serious young woman.

"Ever seen her?" Herd asked.

"No," the man said. "Did she run off on you?"

"Hell, no," Herd said with disgust. Then his attitude brightened. "She's my only sister and we were separated some years back. The last I knew, she lived not far from here, and I'm hoping that somebody will recognize her and know where she went. I'd give anything to meet up with her again."

"Can't help you," the man said. "But I wish you luck."

"Thank you kindly," Herd said, and put the case back in his pocket. "I'm sure I'll run across her eventually. It just wouldn't be right if I didn't."

13

July 1861

I T WAS HOT and Zachary watered Raven at the trough before hitching him to a rail in front of the dry goods store on the square in Harrisonville. Since Frank had left to become an adjutant in Blair's command at St. Louis, Patrick and Zachary took turns making the fifteen-mile journey every two or three weeks, so as not to leave the farm short-handed if trouble arose. They traded with the merchants for what necessities the farm could not produce on its own—salt and flour, mostly, powder and lead— and they seldom failed to pick up a bright piece of cloth or an illustrated magazine or some other nonsense for the girls.

In the dry goods store Zachary's slung shotgun looked odd as he examined the array of ribbon, but he made no apologies. Finally he settled on a shining yellow that reminded him of the color of Sarah's hair in the sunshine, and he placed his nickels on the counter. He was careful to have the purchase divided into equal parts and put into three separate envelopes. As he was tucking the bundle into the saddle wallet thrown over Raven's back, there came the rush of hooves at the end of the street and Zachary looked up to see a column of blue-coated cavalry swarm into the square.

The column roused only mild curiosity in Zachary. Since the beginning of the war there had been plenty of federal soldiers passing through the county—and a smattering of pro-slavery State Guard as well—but there had been no skirmishing, and Harrisonville itself harbored few secessionists. Too late did Zachary notice the telltale red morocco leggings that identified the company as the Seventh Kansas Cavalry—Jennison's Jayhawkers. In the parlance of the border, to jayhawk was to imitate the behavior of the common bluejay—to fight, quarrel, disrupt, and steal from the nests of others, and to generally create havoc. Perhaps the most hated Jayhawker of them all was Charles R. "Doc" Jennison, the leader of the Seventh Cavalry, and today Jennison had brought his Redlegs to Harrisonville.

For a moment Zachary was frozen, unsure of whether to stay where he was beside Raven or to swing into the saddle and make a mad dash for the country. He was painfully aware of the shotgun slung over his shoulder, and decided that running would just give the Jayhawkers an excuse to shoot him. So, calmly as possible, he continued to cinch down the saddlebags while letting the shotgun slide down his arm to the ground, where he kicked it beneath the wooden porch of the storefront.

The troop broke into detachments and with shouts and curses began shooting out shop windows around the square. The residents were held at the point of cocked guns while the Jayhawkers carried cash and merchandise away and wrecked the shops.

Jennison, wearing a brace of Navy colts in his belt and cradling a Sharps rifle, was directing the pillage from atop his horse. He was a small man with pinched eyes that seemed to take in everything between blinks. He directed his men to the Younger's Livery Stable, where dozens of horses and a caravan of buggies and wagons were pressed into service to haul away the loot.

Then the troops broke out the window of the dry goods store and surged inside, forcing the clerk at gunpoint to hand over the cash box. It rankled Zachary that the nickels he had just spent were in that box.

"That's a fine horse," Jennison called to his men, and he indicated Raven with a wave of the barrel of the Sharps. "Liberate it."

Zachary had his foot in the stirrup and was swinging into the saddle by the time Jennison had finished the command, but not before a particularly fat Redleg managed to grab Raven's bit. The horse attempted to rear but screamed in pain as the man put all of his weight into the bit. If Zachary had not already kicked the shotgun beneath the boardwalk he would have blown the man's head off.

"Let go of my horse, you fat bastard," Zachary said, leaning over Raven's neck and hitting the man squarely between the eyes. The man released the bit and dropped to his knees.

Jennison rode in close and jammed Raven while two other Redlegs on foot pressed hard against Zachary's knees, grasping at his trousers. Zachary kicked one of them in the face, sending him sprawling, and pulled back hard on the reins to get Raven turned around. Zachary turned his head to see what was on Raven's flank as Jennison grasped the Sharps by the barrel and swung the gun at his head.

The rifle butt clipped Zachary above the left ear. He felt as if he had been kicked out of the saddle by a mule. He fell and landed face-down in the street, the taste of his own blood filling his mouth.

Raven reared, lashing out with his hooves, and one of his kicks broke the collarbone of one of the Jayhawkers. One wearing sergeant stripes rushed in, but the big black horse bolted before he could grab the reins. Raven raced from the square and disappeared down the hill.

"Damn it," Jennison muttered. "That was a fine horse. What's your name, boy?"

Zachary had struggled to his hands and knees, but he refused to look up. From the corner of his eye he could see the barrel of the shotgun beneath the porch. If he lunged, he thought, he might be able to reach it.

"Answer Colonel Jennison," the sergeant said and kicked Zachary in the ribs. "You goddamn *secesh.*"

"I ain't no sessionist," he said. "My name is Zachary Fenn of the Little Shannon Valley and my father was a Union man who wanted a peaceable end to the slavery question. My brother Frank is with Blair in St. Louis. You Jayhawkers ain't nothin' but robbers and thieves and you don't deserve to wear that uniform you got on."

The sergeant was a big man with a full beard and a knife scar across one cheekbone and he kicked Zachary again. Zachary doubled over, feeling as if his insides were about to come out his mouth. He could almost feel the wood and metal of the shotgun in his hands, it was so close.

"Fenn," Jennison said. "Remember that name, Sergeant Gibbs. It is one worth watching. The boy is obviously lying about his family's secessionist sympathies. These farmers lean on their hoes and deny knowing anything about the enemy during the day while giving aid and comfort to them at night."

"Yes, sir," the sergeant said. "Fenn, sir."

"The boy ought to be shot for resisting arrest and attempting to conceal property," Jennison said. "But he is young and I am in a generous mood. Tie him to the rail and give him twenty lashes with the bullwhip."

Jennison nudged his horse forward.

They tied Zachary's hands around the post while the sergeant put on his gloves and uncoiled the whip. It snaked out upon the ground like a living thing.

"Who's going to count?" the sergeant asked.

"I'll count," the soldier with the broken collarbone said. He was grimacing and holding his shoulder at an awkward angle.

They tore Zachary's shirt away to expose his bare back. The sergeant drew the whip back, letting it unroll behind him, then threw his shoulder into it. The whip lashed out with a crack and carved a long diagonal furrow across Zachary's back. He bit his lower lip to keep from crying out.

"One," the soldier said.

The whip lashed out again and bit another strip of flesh away.

"One," the soldier said again.

Ten more times the whip cracked, and ten more times did the soldier with the broken collarbone count it as "one." Zachary's back felt as if it were on fire, and the hot blood curled down from his rib cage to sprinkle the dirt. Zachary had never hated before, had never truly understood the meaning of the word, but with each lash his understanding increased until he embraced hatred as one would a lover. With each lash his hatred for the Jayhawkers grew, and there was a special place in the depth of his hate for Jennison. The pain grew intolerable and Zachary arched his back and fought against the post like some animal caught in a trap. He no longer stifled his cries but his cries were screams of rage, not of pain.

"Two." The soldier began the count in earnest with the eleventh lash, and by the time the sergeant had made it to "twenty," Zachary hung limply from his bound wrists around the post. His back was a mass of lacerations and in places the skin hung in bloody strips.

"Cut him down," the sergeant said, massaging his tired shoulder.

"We ought to let him hang there," the soldier said.

"A man can't breathe hanging from his arms," the sergeant said matter-of-factly. "He would die, and that's not what Jennison ordered. Cut him loose."

The soldier slipped a knife between Zachary's wrists and severed the rawhide. Zachary fell like a sack of meat on his back into the street, grinding dirt into his wounds. He had remained conscious but unable to speak for the last ten lashes, but the pain of falling onto his back fired his rage anew.

"Jennison," he muttered between dry lips.

The sergeant was surprised he could speak.

"Yes, boy," he said. "What about Colonel Jennison?"

"He should have . . . killed me."

"I'm sure you wish you were dead," the soldier laughed.

"No . . ."

The sergeant understood what Zachary meant, and he was suddenly afraid. These bastards always had brothers or cousins or even womenfolk who would be only too willing to send a ball into you when your back was turned. His hand fingered the butt of the revolver at his belt for a moment, and then he pulled the weapon out and leveled it at Zachary's head.

"Sergeant Gibbs!" Jennison commanded from the courthouse lawn, forty yards away. "Put it away. I told you to flog him, not kill him."

"But, sir—"

"No, sergeant. Put it away. I need your help here to interrogate some suspects in the county offices."

"Yes, sir," the sergeant said, and holstered his revolver. He told the other men to come along. The fat soldier kicked Zachary in the short ribs as he walked past, and the man with the broken collarbone took Zachary's money wallet. A few minutes later another Jayhawker found Zachary lying unconscious and relieved him of his boots.

The town was sacked by the time Major Van Dorn's main body arrived in Harrisonville. Van Dorn was using the Jayhawkers as an advance guard in his campaign to secure the Cass County seat, which was supposedly held by home guard units, but not a single

Confederate soldier was found in the town. The regular troops were disgusted to find what the Jayhawkers had done, and Captain George Caleb Bingham in particular was horrified that Jennison's band of thieves had been afforded the legitimacy of a federal military commission. An artist by trade, Bingham would later use his talents to portray the cruelty of the federal military presence in Missouri.

14

JIM YOUNGER carried Zachary from the street and hid him in his father's livery stable before Van Dorn's main force arrived. Jim, who was just a year younger than Zachary, had known the Fenns all of his life. His older brother, Cole, was with the State Guard and had helped whip the Yankees a few days ago at Carthage. Like Francis Fenn had been, Colonel Henry Younger was staunchly pro-Union, but that had not stopped the Jayhawkers from stealing thousands of dollars in horses and wagons from the stable. Jim knew that it just as easily could have been him instead of Zach that the Jayhawkers whipped like a mule.

Zachary lay unconscious on his stomach in the livery stable for the rest of that day and most of the next while the Youngers cleaned and dressed his wounds. When he finally came to terrible consciousness he asked about his horse, and was relieved that the animal had been caught.

"I don't know what Jennison wanted with him," Jim said. "We had to lead him all the way back here because he won't let anybody ride him but you."

On the third day the Youngers drove Zachary to his home in the back of a wagon. Caitlin knew something terrible must have happened—news of the Jayhawker's raid spread quickly—and when she saw the slow-moving wagon with Zach's riderless horse walking behind she assumed the worst. When she found that Zachary was alive she thanked God for answering her prayers, but she cried when she studied the condition of Zachary's back.

"I'll heal," Zachary told her cheerfully as they carried him inside, but his face betrayed the depth of his pain. The wounds had become infected and fever had taken hold, and Zachary shook with chills and often remarked how cold it was for the middle of July.

When two more days had passed and Zachary had shown no signs of recovery, Uncle Fitz and Patrick set out for Trading Post to fetch Sarah. It was an unhappy journey and Fitz rode with his rifle across his lap. Patrick was keenly aware of the weight of the Colt tucked into his belt and he told Fitz that he would personally kill Jennison if Zachary died. Fitz shook his head and said it was bad luck even to speak of the boy dying. At Trading Post they told Sarah the news, and with no tears but great haste, she packed a few things and climbed into the wagon.

Sarah sat by Zachary's bed and held his hand while the fever raged, letting go only to mop his brow or to change the bedding or to clean the wounds. She talked to him in a cheerful voice and discussed a hundred ordinary things that they would do once they had a home of their own, but not once did he seem to hear her. She slept in a chair beside the bed and early on the morning of the sixth day the fever broke. Zachary opened his eyes and was amazed to find Sarah asleep beside the bed.

He watched her while she slept and when she roused he asked her gently if he could have a little water and some breakfast, that he was powerfully hungry. She pressed his head to her breast and cried for the first time, and told him how afraid she had been of losing him.

"You can't get rid of a Fenn that easy," Zachary said. "We're like a bad habit—we always come back."

Sarah stayed at the Little Shannon Valley and as Zachary grew stronger they sat together in the yard during the cool of the evening. Every so often Jim Younger would come by to see how Zachary was faring, and he and Zach would talk in low voices about the Union military occupation. After Governor Jackson had called for 50,000 men to resist the Union invasion, General Nathaniel Lyon (another Kansan) drove the governor and the legislature out of Jefferson City and installed his own provisional, pro-Union government. At the same time he seized control of the waterways and the state's railroads. Governor Jackson and the uprooted state legislature landed in Neosho, in southwest Missouri, and were desperately trying to pass an ordinance of secession to make Mis-

souri the twelfth star in the Confederate battle flag. Closer to
home, the Jayhawkers had remained in Kansas since the depreda-
tion visited on Harrisonville, but nerves remained taut. At any
time, Jennison—or Lane, the "grim chieftain," or the religious
fanatic James Montgomery—could sally across the border to loot
and murder with impunity.

Jenny, who by now was growing quite large with the baby,
wrote Frank in St. Louis about what had happened and Frank
promised to take it up with General Fremont, who had replaced
Blair. Unfortunately Fremont himself was soon to be replaced and
there were dozens of reports already filtering in from the border.
Frank wrote Jenny about how discouraging the situation was in
St. Louis, and how much better he would feel if he could only test
himself in battle, rather than being lost in a mountain of paper-
work. The war was going badly in the East and the Union command was so cautious that it had become impotent, a contagion
that spread down from the very general-in-chief of the Union
armies, George B. McClellan. Despite the gunplay along the old
Sante Fe Trail that had felled the Herd cousins—which had more
to do with reflexes than courage—Frank still secretly wondered if
he was a coward. He longed to "see the elephant" for himself, as
federal recruits called the baptism of fire. The only action that
Frank had witnessed to date was a bit of street fighting while
Union soldiers were marching a captured State Guard unit into
St. Louis. A pro-Southern mob attacked the column and the federal troops fired into the crowd, killing several women and children. The slaughter, Frank wrote, had sickened him.

As the war progressed Uncle Fitz became increasingly restless.
His views on war had not changed since he had taken to the
mountains to escape the war with Mexico in the 1840s, and in fact
they had deepened: never had the Fenns owned a single slave,
and if the Southern states wanted to leave the Union, that was
their business; Fitz would take no sides in this pissing contest over
the Mason-Dixon Line between ungainly Abe Lincoln and tired
old Jeff Davis. But if he stayed in Cass County, he was afraid
somebody would choose his sides for him, as they had done for
poor Zachary. Fitz had already stayed longer than he had intended, out of concern for Caitlin and pregnant Jenny, and he
wished Frank would just come home and put an end to this foolishness.

August burned away like a slow fuse while life on the farm continued as best it could. Patrick found himself working harder than he had ever believed possible, to make up for the loss of manpower while Zachary healed and Frank was absent. He came to resent the farm as a burden that he had never asked for. Zachary spent more and more time with Jim Younger and other of the young men from the county, and they looked over their shoulders while they talked furtively of the war. Zachary was delighted when Price and McCullough outnumbered and defeated Union forces at the Battle of Wilson's Creek, where Lyon was shot dead from the saddle. Zachary did not consider that Lyon had worn the same color uniform as his brother, Frank; what mattered to Zachary was that Lyon was a Kansan, and that all Kansans were hated.

15

September 1861

ON THE MORNING that Jenny went into labor, the fields of the Little Shannon Valley were overrun by five hundred Union soldiers chasing a one-hundred-man State Guard unit. The cornfields that surrounded the house took on strategic importance as the State Guard used their cover to snipe at the advancing federals. When a butternut-clad sharpshooter knocked Colonel Johnson from his horse, the federals began to systematically trample down every stalk of corn. Those crops that were not destroyed by design were crushed by sheer confusion, as even the wheat and the oats were ground under heel by alternately frightened or exhilarated soldiers. Even Caitlin's vegetable garden beside the barn, the turnips and beets and melons and the flowers that were useless save for table decoration, were trampled.

Zachary watched the battle from the roof of the barn until his Uncle Fitz hollered for him to come into the safety of the house. Never had he seen so many men with guns, and never had he seen so many poor shots. Both sides had put enough lead in the air to kill off a town twice the size of Harrisonville, but few balls found their mark. The ragged State Guard, dressed predominantly in homespun and carrying weapons that ranged from revolving pistols to squirrel rifles, were the better shots but they were hopelessly outnumbered and weary after being cut off and chased through three counties. The Union soldiers were outfitted well with their blue uniforms and bedrolls and big-bore Enfield rifles, but they seemed to load and fire without regard to taking aim. To Zachary, the federal force seemed like one huge scattergun that sprayed the fields ahead of it.

It was these errant shots that worried Zachary as he sprinted from the barn to the back door of the house, and not a few minié balls left puffs in the ground around him as he ran. Inside there was confusion as well. The federals had turned the home into a field hospital and they had laid the unfortunate Colonel Johnson on a pallet in the middle of the kitchen floor. His jacket had been removed and his shirt cut away to reveal a chest wound that made a terrible sucking sound at each breath. There was little the surgeon could do for him except administer morphine in order to ease his passage.

Every so often Jenny would scream upstairs.

The surgeon's immediate attention was on a soldier who lay on the kitchen table. His knee had been shattered and while three men held the injured man down, the surgeon went to work to finish the job by sawing away his leg. The man screamed piteously and when the surgeon had finished he threw the severed limb into a bucket. Blood covered the kitchen floor and Zachary studied the way it pooled and ran along the baseboards until it disappeared in the cracks to sprinkle down in the cellar.

"Captain," an orderly said, leaning over the stairs and calling into the kitchen. "There's a woman up here that's having the devil's own time bringing a baby, and her sister wants to know if you'd lend a hand."

"Yes, I'll be there directly," the surgeon said, washing his hands in a pail of rose-colored water. "Babies do pick the damnedest times to come into this world, don't they?" The surgeon wiped his hands on his apron and turned to speak cheerfully to the colonel, but the man had already died. The surgeon leaned gently over and closed the man's eyes.

He noticed Zachary standing by the stove.

"Boy, you'd better get down into the cellar with the others," the surgeon said. "With the way you're dressed, some of the men are likely to think you're with the rebels."

"What's wrong with the way I'm dressed?" Zachary asked indignantly.

"Never mind, boy. Just go."

"That's my sister-in-law up there having that baby," Zachary said, "and I reckon I'm going to stick around until it comes. This is my house and I'll be damned if I'm going to take orders from a Yankee."

"I'm not a Yankee, boy, I'm a surgeon," the man said. "Hell, I feel more like the angel of death than anything. Any other time, and they would call this murder. And this meaningless skirmish that took this good man's life won't even have a name."

He looked at Zachary, and he saw it was lost on the boy.

"But you're right, it's your house and your family. Come upstairs and you can sit outside the door, if you've a mind to. Maybe I can feel a little bit like the life-giver I thought I was going to be when I was young."

The surgeon grabbed his bag and Zachary followed him up the stairs to the room where Jenny lay. When the man opened the door Zachary got a peek inside. Jenny was lying in bed with the sheet half off her and her knees sticking up, and her face was an angry red and her lips were drawn back from her teeth. She was sweating fiercely. Caitlin sat beside her, holding her hand tight in her own.

"Thank God," Caitlin said when she saw the man's bag. "I'm afraid the baby is turned, doctor, and Jenny is having a terrible time."

Then the door shut and Zachary sat down with his back against the wall and he hugged his knees and listened. He could hear the surgeon speaking low and quickly to Caitlin, and comfortingly to Jenny, and then there were no more sounds for a while. Outside, the pop of rifles continued sporadically as the last of the State Guard was routed. After what seemed much too long he heard Jenny laughing—or was it crying?—and then the sharp report of a slap, and finally the squeal of a newborn.

The door opened and Zachary got to his feet.

"Take a look," the doctor said. The baby was wrapped in a cloth and lay, pink and helpless, in Jenny's arms. "You have a nephew."

"A boy," Zachary said.

Caitlin nodded.

"What's its name?"

"*His* name," Caitlin said, "is Francis Fenn the third, and will you please shut the door quietly and go tell Uncle Fitz and Patrick that Jenny is weak but that she and the baby are fine."

"Frank will be proud," Zachary said, and shut the door.

Zachary went down the stairs and through the kitchen to get to the cellar, but he paused beside the body of the dead colonel. There was a wedding ring on his left hand. He looked back up, toward where Jenny and the baby lay, and he thought about what the surgeon had said earlier.

"I'll give it a name," Zachary said. "From now on, this'll be called the Battle of the Corn, and I'll always remember it because it was the day that Little Frank was born. And I'm sorry, colonel whoever you are, I surely am."

The soldiers pulled out as quickly as they had come, but they managed to take just about everything of value that was left on the farm. Hams were thrown over shoulders, chickens killed, bags of flour and salt and coffee carried away. The horses and furniture were spared only because they were too large for an enlisted man to stuff in his knapsack.

Zachary knew the situation was grim without having to talk it over with the others. None of them had eaten all day and his own stomach was beginning to complain, and he especially worried about Jenny and the baby. Caitlin gathered up the remains of the garden and made a thin vegetable soup, but it was not enough to sustain them for very long. The army had run off all of the game, and it would be a while before so much as a rabbit could be had in the Little Shannon Valley; besides, a man didn't want to take a gun into the woods until things simmered down.

Zachary reflected on all this and toward sundown he took the shotgun and saddled Raven and told Patrick he was going to visit the neighbors and ask to borrow some food. Patrick offered to come with him, but Zachary said he'd best go alone.

He rode south, in the direction the Union soldiers had taken. They were on foot, and in no hurry to actually overrun the State Guard, so they hadn't gone far. Zachary crested a hill and found the light from their campfires dotting a field along the old dragoon trace, not seven miles from the Little Shannon Valley.

It was a moonless night and Zachary kept to the timber while he studied the camp. The tents were pitched in orderly rows and the guns were stacked nearby. There was fiddle music and laughter and other foolishness, and the smell of ham and beans cooking over the open fires. The officers' horses were tied to a picket line to the south, alongside the quartermaster's wagons and the two field guns with caissons. Pickets had been placed around the perimeter of the camp, but each were so noisy and clumsy that their positions were obvious.

Zachary dismounted and held the reins in his hand while he thought. There was no use blundering into the camp, even if the Yankees were poor shots, because there were just too many of them and he would be a cooked goose sure. It was no good to ambush one of the pickets, because they weren't likely to have much on them. No, he decided, he would have to position himself along the old dragoon road—maybe at the bridge where it crossed the creek—and take his chances at whatever came along.

The bridge was a mile from the camp and crossed a shallow creek with deep cut banks, too deep for a horse to climb. Zachary rode back and forth across the bridge, studying the terrain, and finally he decided on a cluster of trees near the south end of the bridge. He tied a kerchief over his face and waited.

After more than an hour Zachary heard the rumble of a wagon coming down the old road, and his hands tightened on the grip of the shotgun. Through the trees he could see the ghost of its canvas top approaching. It seemed to take forever for the wagon to reach the bridge, and all the while Zachary's heart was in his throat. When Zachary heard the iron-rimmed wheels on the planks, he told himself it was time to spring, but he couldn't force himself to move.

Oh, hell, he thought, *it's buck fever.*

He watched silently as the military wagon and its escort of half a dozen riders passed by. He was thankful that he hadn't charged out. There was no telling how many guns would have been instantly brought to bear on him, and he didn't even know whether there was anything in the wagon worth stealing. *This highwayman business,* he allowed, *might take a little more study.*

He nudged Raven onto the road and headed north, toward the river, where he could sit and think.

Patrick was up long before first light, and he worked quietly and quickly as he packed his saddlebags and threw what clothes he had into a grain sack. He had finally made up his mind to leave while sitting in the cellar and watching the blood drip down from the cracks in the kitchen floor. He wasn't a coward—he would take any man on, barefisted, toe-to-toe, but this wasn't his fight; there wasn't anybody in the world he felt strong enough about to kill, and he sure as hell didn't want anybody killing him. But it didn't take much smarts to figure out that somebody was going to force him to join one army or the other. He was twenty years old now, and he wanted to live to see twenty-one. He was going out West to sit out the war.

Patrick threw the saddlebags over his shoulder and, carrying the sack of clothes, walked down the stairs to where Uncle Fitz was asleep in front of the fireplace. He knelt down and tapped Fitz on the shoulder, and the old man's eyes opened quickly.

"It's just me," Patrick said.

"Are you leaving now?" Fitz asked. He knew what had been on the boy's mind, even though Patrick had not spoken a word of it.

"This war ain't for me," Patrick said. "I'm headed out. I'm going to be a trapper and I aim to reach the Powder River, maybe farther. I've come to ask if you want to come with me."

Fitz blinked.

"I'm afraid not," he said.

"You're not too old—"

"It ain't that, boy," Fitz said, shaking his head. "It's what's sleeping upstairs right now. I can't leave these three girls and that baby alone. You do what you have to do—Lord knows, I did when I was your age. But you remember that you're a Fenn, and that you've got family, and that one day we expect you back."

Patrick nodded. He squeezed his uncle's shoulder and got to his feet.

"You're forgettin' something," Fitz said.

"What's that?"

"Your rifle. You can't expect to survive in the mountains without a decent rifle." Fitz motioned to his .50-caliber Hawken, which was leaned against the wall for the night. "Take it. Take the damn bag with it. There's plenty of powder and shot, and a fair amount of lead."

"Fitz, I can't."

"Take it, damn you," Fitz said. "There's nobody else I would trust it to."

Patrick nodded and added the rifle and pouch to his load. At the door he turned and said, "I want you to know I'm just borrowing it." Then he walked out to the barn, saddled Deadhead, and rode off.

· · · ·

Dawn found Zachary still sitting on his haunches alongside the south fork of the Grand River and he watched without joy as the sun rose. His gut hurt and there seemed to be a fire behind his eyes. He had been motionless for so long that when he stood his knee joints popped and he had to rub his legs for a few minutes to restore the circulation. Presently he slung the shotgun over his shoulder and mounted Raven, waiting patiently where Zachary had dropped the reins. He crested the riverbank and picked up the road that led toward Harrisonville.

Early morning fog clung to the river valley and he rode through the mist at an easy trot for twenty minutes. Presently he heard the clatter of a wagon coming toward him, and he slipped the kerchief over his face. The fog was so thick he didn't see the wagon until it was twenty yards away. It was a government mail coach, probably bound for Pleasant Hill, with a two-horse team and a pair of soldiers up front. The teamster was an older man with corporal's stripes and did not appear to be armed, although the soldier sitting next to him had a carbine upright between his knees. Zachary did not yield the road and the teamster reined his horses to a stop just a few feet from Raven's nose.

"Get out of the goddamned road," the teamster said.

Zachary unslung the shotgun and cocked both hammers. He ordered the men to throw down their weapons.

"What the hell is this, a robbery?"

Zachary put the shotgun on his hip and aimed it at the teamster's chest. "You have exactly two seconds to throw down your arms or I'm going to give each of you a taste of this scattergun."

The soldier with the carbine dropped it weakly onto the road and the teamster disgustedly pulled a revolver, barrel first, from beneath his jacket and pitched it over the side.

"Are you two alone?"

"Yeah, we're alone," the teamster said. "There's not enough troops in the state of Missouri to provide an escort for every mail coach that's bound for some backwater town. All they give me is Tom here, and you can see what a fireball he is. He thought you was a ghost, so quick did you come out of the fog. Say, you ain't going to kill us, are you?"

"How come the other one doesn't talk?"

"Tom never talks," the teamster said. "You didn't answer me about whether you were going to kill us or not."

"I won't kill you as long as you keep doing what I say. Do you have any food?"

"See there, Tom? Ghosts don't need no food," the teamster said. "We got a little with us. We got a bucket here with some salt pork and some chicken and a few biscuits that are harder than a goddamned rock."

"Any money?"

"There's some in the box behind the seat. It's postal money."

"Good," Zachary said. "Now climb down from there and do it easy. Come stand in front of me."

They did. Tom's face was rigid, and his eyes were big. "You're going to shoot us now, ain't you?" he asked.

"Take off your shoes," Zachary said, "and empty your pockets."

"Goddamn," the teamster said.

They placed their belongings together with their shoes in a pile in the middle of the road.

"Now, take off," Zachary said.

"Which way?" the quiet soldier asked.

"Any way you like, but do it fast. And if there's any trouble over this, if I find a squad of Yankee soldiers on my tail, I will find you somehow and kill you both."

"Goddamn," the teamster said. "Come on, Tom."

They started off at a trot back up the road to Harrisonville.

Zachary dismounted, climbed into the wagon, and found the bucket of food and the locked cash box. The coach was full of mail and official-looking packages, and suddenly, flushing with anger, he slung armfuls out into the road. He stopped when he realized the job would take too long. He climbed back down from the coach, picked up the revolver that the teamster had dropped, and slid it into his belt. Then he picked through the pile of things in the road, picking up the greenbacks and the coins and a pocket watch. He also found a key for the cash box, and he opened the box and scooped the money out of it. There appeared to be over a hundred dollars in notes and coins, and this he deposited in a saddlebag.

Then he cocked the revolver and fired it into the air near the team. The horses bolted and the mail coach shot off down the road, letters flying out of the back. Raven took a few nervous steps backward, but did not run. Zachary picked the carbine from the road, considered keeping it, then realized he had too much to carry. He threw the gun as far into the woods as he could sling it.

Finally Zachary picked up the bucket of food and swung awkwardly into the saddle. His head was pounding and the fire behind his eyes had gotten worse. He lowered his kerchief, nudged Raven in the flanks, and started for home.

16

March 1862

BILL QUANTRILL took off his black slouch hat and sat down in the straight-backed wooden chair in the center of the barn. He tipped the chair backward until it rested lightly against the post behind him, then he stuck a cigar in the corner of his mouth and called for a light. George Todd struck a lucifer match against the post and offered the flame in cupped hands while Quantrill puffed the cigar to life.

Todd hung a lantern from a peg and adjusted the wick until the area was bathed in light. Quantrill ran his fingers through his tangled hair and reflected that a visit to the barber was long overdue. But then, he had been busy since he and fifteen of the boys had ridden into Independence and run head-on into a column of Union cavalry. Quantrill was as surprised as the troopers, but instead of quailing he had placed the reins in his teeth and charged the group with a revolver in each hand. Two of the boys were killed that day, and Quantrill took a ball in the leg, but for sheer audaciousness it was hard to beat. Although his leg still pained him some, Quantrill had remained in the brush, eluding Yankee patrols and generally creating hell. His command was gathering recruits every day, it seemed, from the ranks of farm boys who were chafing under the Yankee bit. Tonight they had slipped down into Cass County and camped in the back lot of a sympathetic farmer named Sears. Tomorrow, Quantrill planned to swing back north into Clay and Jackson Counties and bedevil the Yankees.

"Bill, there's a lady and a boy outside wanting to see you," Todd said. "Should I let them in?"

"George, you should never keep a woman waiting," Quantrill said, his hand resting idly on the butt of one of the two Colt revolvers in his belt. "Show her in."

The woman entered, pushing a boy in front of her. She was a farmer's wife, judging from her plain dress, and the boy wore homespun and couldn't have been more than fourteen years old. His ears seemed too big for his head and freckles covered the bridge of his nose.

"Do you mind if I smoke?" Quantrill asked, suddenly becoming self-conscious in the presence of a woman. He flicked the dust from his red shirt and his dove-colored trousers. "I'll put it out, if you like."

"No, sir, you go right ahead," the woman said in a shaky voice. "My Chester used to smoke a cigar now and again and I didn't mind."

"Thank you."

"Mr. Quantrill," she said, "my name is Amanda Crawford, and this here is my only son. His name is Riley and his father was shot dead by the Jayhawkers last month on the front porch of our home in Blue Springs. Chester was a good man and—" The woman stopped and wiped her eyes with the sleeve of her dress. "They shot him down like a dog, a common dog, for trying to save our mules by hiding them in the woods. Then they burned the house to the ground. Now I can't provide for myself, much less Riley. I'd like for Riley to join your company, Mr. Quantrill, and learn to be a soldier and to avenge the death of his father."

"What do you want, Riley?" Quantrill asked.

The boy answered immediately: "I want to kill Yankees, sir." His eyes were hard and brown, with none of the mirth of childhood.

"I imagine you'll do," Quantrill said. "Do you have a gun?"

"No, sir. The Jayhawkers took Pa's rifle."

Quantrill nodded, then called for his lieutenant. "George, find this recruit and his mother some food, and see if we can't locate a gun for this young man. I believe we took some Sharps from that recruiting office in Liberty."

Todd nodded, then asked: "Aren't you going to make him pledge the oath?"

"George, this boy's oath is written in his eyes."

Quantrill took a ten-dollar gold piece from his shirt and pressed it into the woman's palm.

"This is for you. You take care of yourself, now."

"Thank you, Mr. Quantrill," Mrs. Crawford said, wringing his hand. "I won't forget you for this. Pardon my language, but you give them Yankees hell, you understand?"

"Yes, ma'am," Quantrill said. "I reckon we will."

Todd saw the woman and the boy to the door of the barn, and directed one of the men outside to get them a plate of the stew that was cooking over the fire.

"Bill, there's somebody else to see you," George said. "A farm boy. You want me to let him in?"

"What the hell is it this time?"

"Another recruit, I expect," Todd said.

"Send him in."

Zachary Fenn walked into the barn. His hair was down to his shoulders and he wore a black guerrilla shirt that Sarah had spent a week making. The shirt was loose, with big pockets on each breast, and it was decorated with bits of red and yellow embroidery and gathered in the front by a rosette. Into a wide leather belt were tucked a skinning knife and a .36-caliber Navy revolver. His gray pants were stuffed into a pair of black U.S. Army cavalry boots.

The twenty-four-year-old guerrilla leader chewed on the stub of his cigar and looked Zachary over.

"Where'd you get those boots?" Quantrill asked.

"I stole them off a Union lieutenant after I had him leave his clothes in the middle of the road and made him take off runnin'," Zachary said. "Where'd you get yours?"

Quantrill looked down at his brown boots.

"I pulled mine off a dead Jayhawker I shot in the face at Blue Springs," he said. "The man had struck a farmer's wife across the face, and I allowed that he could try it with me. It was a happy circumstance that his feet were my size."

Quantrill held out a cigar.

"No," Zachary said. "I don't smoke."

"Do you drink?"

"Not that either."

"I see," Quantrill said. "What is it you want?"

"My name's Zachary Fenn and I'm from the Little Shannon Valley, a ways to the west. After Jennison had me whipped on the square in Harrisonville and the Yankees ruined our crops last year, I robbed a mail coach. I held up a Yankee supply wagon just before Christmas and another on New Year's, and yesterday I caught the lieutenant and his escort on the road to Independence. Things have gotten pretty warm for me of recent. Jim Younger tells me that his brother Cole joined your outfit after the Yankees killed their Pa, and there's been lots of talk of you in the county. I reckon I either have to leave Cass County or join up with you."

"That's good," Quantrill said. "What do they say about me?"

"That you're not afraid of a fight."

Quantrill nodded.

"Can you ride and can you shoot?" he asked.

"I'll put myself against any man you've got," Zachary said. "I can shoot straight with my horse at a dead run, and there ain't nobody got a better or smarter animal than mine. I hate all Kansans and have sworn to turn the tables on the Jayhawkers, and I reckon you can help me do it."

"You're a mite sure of yourself," Quantrill said.

"There's no brag there. You can try me if you like."

"There's no need of us killing each other," Quantrill said easily. "We'll save it for the Yankees. Will you take the black oath?"

"What is that?"

"Will you swear to follow orders, to be true to your fellows, and to kill those who serve and support the Union?"

"By God," Zachary said, "I swear it."

It wasn't until after Zachary had tied his horse to the picket line outside and spread his bedroll on the cold ground that he realized he had sworn to kill his brother Frank.

The next day they raided an army recruiting post at Liberty and captured eight Union soldiers—to whom Quantrill gave field paroles on the spot—and, a week later, burned the Blue River bridge on the road from Independence to Kansas City. The toll keeper and a sergeant assigned to the bridge were shot. Quantrill had just read in the papers that General Halleck had issued an order from St. Louis that all guerrillas were to be considered outlaws and that, if captured, they would not be dealt with as prisoners of war, but would be publicly hung as robbers and murderers. Until Quantrill read the papers, it was his policy to release captured Yankee soldiers on a field parole, in which they swore to lay down their arms and never take them up again. At the bridge, Quantrill shot the Union sergeant himself, remarking that the rules of the game were such that no quarter could be given. From that time on, no prisoners were taken and no field paroles offered.

Quantrill's hundred men were more than sufficient to accomplish the raids on the recruiting post and the bridge, and Zachary did little more than to ride alongside and brandish his pistol. It all seemed ridiculously easy to Zach, and in a moment of bravado he told Quantrill he was bored.

The night following the bridge burning, Zach was among the twenty-six men that made camp with Quantrill at a farm owned by David Tate in Jackson County; the remaining three quarters of the command scattered to take refuge with friends or relatives and planned to regroup later. The guerrillas had barely settled in for the night when one of the scouts spotted a detachment of blue-coated cavalry approaching the farm.

Major James Pomeroy of the Second Kansas had his men surround the farmhouse, and then he dismounted and walked up to the house with a warrant for Tate's arrest tucked under his arm. No sooner had Pomeroy rapped on the door than a blast splintered its lower half and a rifle ball shattered one of the major's legs. As the careless major crawled away, his soldiers directed a fusillade at the house.

Zachary was sitting on the floor with his back to the wall and his pistol in his hand. The house was brick, except for an addition out back, but plenty of rounds were coming in through the windows and were chewing up the interior of the Tate's house, smashing dishes and breaking mirrors and splintering furniture. Tate's wife and children were huddled in the kitchen and they screamed in terror as the house seemed to burst around them.

Quantrill had a pistol in each hand and was pacing in a circle in the center of the dining room frantically. His blue eyes were blazing and he seemed strangely animated by the very desperateness of the situation. Finally he jerked the white cloth from the table and, wrapping a broken dish inside it, pitched it out one of the front windows. The firing slackened and finally stopped.

"We ain't giving up," Quantrill shouted, standing beside the window with his back to the wall, "but there's women and children in here, for God's sake. Let them get safely out of here and then we can begin this dance in earnest."

The darkness beyond the window was silent for a moment, and then a voice called back that they would hold their fire until the noncombatants were clear. Quantrill ordered Tate's wife and sister-in-law and their children to leave by the front door, and they lost no time in doing so.

"What do you think now, farm boy?" Quantrill asked as he crouched and checked the loads in his revolvers. "Are you still bored?"

"It is getting a mite interesting," Zachary conceded.

Ten minutes passed as they waited for the troopers to resume the barrage, but none came. Then there were some rustlings toward the back portion of the house, and the telltale smell of coal oil.

The Kansans had set the wooden addition on fire.

"Well, this is a tight spot," Quantrill laughed as flames began licking through the back walls and smoke filled the house. "I guess Dave Tate has lost himself a house. It looks like we either sit in here and suffocate or we run out the front door and give the Yankees a shooting gallery."

"The men are waiting for orders," David Pool said, and then began a coughing fit from the smoke. "The only thing we can do is rush the front."

"No, they're expecting that," Quantrill said, and his eyes danced. "We're going out the back way instead."

Pool quickly called the men from upstairs and rounded up the others, and they crouched together in the kitchen, hiding their faces with their sleeves against the heat of the fire.

"On the count of three," Quantrill called, "we're going to kick the living daylights out of this sorry excuse for a back wall. Remember, there's no chance for us but to fight our way out of here. No quarter asked, boys, and no quarter given!"

"You gotta give Bill credit," one of the men said. "He never runs short of ideas."

"Or guts," another added.

"Ready on the line!" Quantrill called. "One. Two . . . Three!"

With rebel yells sounding from two dozen throats the guerrillas flung themselves at the back wall. It collapsed from their combined force, sending showers of flame and burning wood everywhere. Most of the Kansans were in front, sighted down on the front door. The dozen men stationed in the rear were so taken aback to see a pack of screaming, pistol-waving madmen leaping out of the flames that they ran for their lives.

Zachary shook burning embers from his neck and shoulders and fired the Colt as fast as he could cock the hammer as he ran. Accuracy was not his concern—he just wanted the Yankees to move out of the way.

The fire had the back lot lit up like noon on the Fourth of July and most of the guerrillas dashed for the safety of the dark woods. Two of them fell in mid-stride, felled by shots from the sides of the house, and they landed heavily in the dirt. Zachary hesitated a moment, then joined a handful making for the picket line near the barn, where they had left their horses.

Five Union soldiers guarded the mounts, and this group had time to take aim. The man running beside Zachary was hit in the chest, and Zachary heard a minié ball part the air near his own head. They were upon the horses in a moment. Two of the soldiers were mortally wounded by pistol fire and the others gave. Only the soldier that had fired at Zachary stood his ground and he was desperately trying to reload his cumbersome single-shot rifle, but his hands shook so that he spilled the powder from the paper cartridge and dropped the ball on the ground.

Zachary stuck his revolver a foot from the man's face and pulled the trigger. The hammer snapped on a spent cylinder. Zachary knocked him reeling with the butt of the gun. He pulled Raven loose from the line and swung into the saddle in the same motion.

In a moment he was flying across the dark fields.

17

ZACHARY REACHED HOME the day after the escape at the Tate farm, and he waited in the woods until the sun had gone down and he was sure there were no Union patrols about before he hid Raven in the barn and slipped through the back door.

Caitlin was in the kitchen and she put her hand over her mouth when she saw him. His hair was singed and his face was black with soot from the fire. There were holes burned in his shirt and the fabric was gone from both knees. He had a cut beneath his left eye where a nail had caught him, and blood was caked from his cheekbone to his jaw.

"How bad are you hurt?" Caitlin asked, latching the door behind him.

"Where's Sarah?"

"She's upstairs. We need to get you cleaned and stitched up before that cut turns green. Were you followed?"

"No."

"What am I to say if the Yankees come about?"

"That you haven't seen me in two weeks, that there was bad blood between us when we parted, and that you don't care where I am now. You take any kind of loyalty oath they offer, you hear?"

"I'll just say I haven't seen you," she said. "Sit down on the stool. I imagine you're hungry, too."

"I'm starving," he said.

"We don't have much," Caitlin said.

"Anything will do."

She gave him some day-old cornbread and went upstairs to

fetch Sarah. When they came back down, Zachary was stuffing a piece of cornbread into his mouth with dirty fingers. Sarah tried not to cry when she saw him, but tears escaped from the corners of her eyes and rolled down her cheeks. Zachary held her in his lap and wiped the tears away with rough hands.

"How's Jenny and Little Frank?" Zachary asked after he had spent a few minutes holding Sarah in his arms.

"They're getting along," Caitlin said. "They're both upstairs, asleep."

"Good," he said. "Don't tell her I was here."

"Why not?" Caitlin asked.

"It would just be better if you didn't," Zachary said, feeling the guilt rise up in his chest. Sarah began to cry again when she realized Zachary intended on leaving before Jenny woke up, so he changed the subject.

"It was one helluva fight," Zachary said. "Bill Quantrill is either the bravest or the craziest man I have ever met, I don't know which. You should have seen the look on those Yankee faces when we come kicking and screaming out of that burning house. Precious, it was."

"Were many of you hurt?"

"Just one or two," Zachary lied. "But they got twenty-five of our horses, all of them except Raven. I couldn't leave him behind."

"I read the papers this week," Caitlin said. "You'll hang if they catch you. I want you to think about leaving for a spell, maybe going out West and finding Patrick."

"I can't do that," Zachary said. "This is my home. The country may be run by Yankees, but this is still my home. Besides, how are you all going to get along without me?"

"I'll eat grass if I have to just to know you're safe," Sarah said.

"Don't worry," Zachary said. "I'm not going to let anything happen to me as long as I have you waiting for me."

"Please," Sarah said.

"I'm no coward," Zachary said. "I'm not going to run."

"You'll end up being a dead fool," Cait said. "You know this scar is going to be permanent, don't you?"

"It's nothing," he said.

Zachary took off his guerrilla shirt for Sarah to mend while Caitlin scrubbed his face and hands and tended to his cut. Some greenbacks and coins spilled out of the pockets of the shirt when

Sarah spread it over her lap, and Zachary said it was his share from the Liberty raid, and that it was for them.

"You didn't kill anybody for it, did you?" Caitlin asked. When Zachary said he hadn't she scooped up the money.

"I'm running mighty low on caps," Zachary said. "We get plenty of powder and lead from the Yankees, but the caps they use for their rifles are too big for the nipples on our revolvers. Could you buy me some the next time you go into town?"

"Of course," Caitlin said.

"Get two or three tins."

"But how will we get them to you?" she asked.

"Put them inside the trunk of the oak tree that was hit by lightning, the one on the hill where Ma and Pa are buried," Zachary said. "I'll be back in a fortnight to get them. I'll leave anything I have for you there, too."

The man surprised Jake Herd as he was pawing through the contents of a trunk in the bedroom, and Herd casually pulled his revolver from his belt and aimed it at the man's nose.

"You can save me a lot of trouble," Herd said. "Where's your money?"

"I don't have any money," the farmer stammered, throwing his hands into the air.

"I kill people that don't have money."

Herd cocked the revolver.

"Wait," the man pleaded. "There's a few dollars hidden in a tin beneath the mattress."

"That's more like it," Herd said, and walked to the bed. The war had put Herd out of the slave-stealing business, and for some months he had been breaking into homes and pocketing whatever was worth taking. He had watched this house in Vernon County all day, making sure that it would be unoccupied when he kicked in the door. It was just like a damned farmer, Herd thought, to blunder into the middle of a burglary—and then to ask questions about it.

Herd found the tin and shook the money out into the palm of his hand. Five dollars in notes and less than a dollar in coins. He shook his head.

"That's all?"

"That's all," the farmer said.

Herd took the leather case from his pocket and held the daguerreotype in front of the farmer's face.

"Take a good look," Herd said. "Have you ever seen this woman before?"

The farmer peered at the picture.

"No," he said at length. "She is not familiar to me."

Herd slipped the leather case back in his pocket and shot the farmer in the forehead.

18

THE WINDOWS of the general store in Harrisonville were boarded over so the Jayhawkers wouldn't have anything to break the next time they rode through town. The owner of the store was a man named Wilson and he greeted Caitlin with a smile when she walked through the door.

"How's the family, Miss Fenn?" Wilson asked.

"Fine, thank you," she said, noting with relief that they were alone in the store. "Little Frank is growing like a weed."

"Have you heard from Frank?"

"No, I'm afraid we haven't, but you know how uncertain the mails are these days."

"That's a fact," Wilson said. "You know, there's been no mail from St. Louis in three weeks. I understand that the army can't find volunteers to drive the coaches because of the bushwhackers. What can I do for you today?"

Caitlin produced a list and told him what she needed: a package of needles, some black thread, salt, beans, flour if he had it or cornmeal if he didn't, and three tins of No. 11 percussion caps.

Wilson set about gathering up the items while Caitlin nervously waited at the counter. It seemed to take the man forever as he picked through the items on the sparse shelves to fill her order.

"I'm sorry, but I just have two tins of caps left," Wilson said.

"That will do," Caitlin said, then added with a smile: "They're for my Uncle Fitz. He always likes to have plenty on hand . . . They're for his squirrel rifle."

Wilson nodded and placed the tins on the counter with the rest of the items while he reckoned up her purchase with a pad and pencil. He was as slow at the math as he was in filling her order, and Caitlin tensed when she heard the door open and the sound of boots. A Union officer walked over and leaned on the counter, and he touched the brim of his hat when his eyes met Caitlin's.

"How do you do, Captain," she said, forcing a smile.

"I need a couple plugs of tobacco when you're finished filling this lady's order," the man said. He looked over the items on the counter and picked up one of the tins of percussion caps. "Somebody plan on doing a lot of shooting?" he asked.

"Those are for her uncle," Wilson said.

"Indeed," the captain said.

"Oh, you have reminded me," Caitlin said. "I need a plug of tobacco for my Uncle Fitz as well. My, he would have been angrier than a hornet had I forgotten it."

"If you will forgive me," the captain asked, "may I ask your name?"

"She's Caitlin Fenn," Wilson said before she could speak. "Francis Fenn's daughter. They have a farm down on the south fork of the Grand River. I was sorry to hear about your father's death."

"Thank you," Caitlin said. "I was saddened as well to hear of the death of Colonel Bud Younger. He was a good man and a true friend of Pa's." Younger, owner of the livery stable and the father of Jim and Cole, had been shot dead by a band of Jayhawkers.

"Fenn," the captain said. "I believe we have a warrant for the arrest of a Zachary Fenn. Is he relation to you?"

Wilson was silent this time.

"Indeed," Caitlin said with a smile. "Zachary is my brother. What on earth would you want to arrest Zachary for?"

"Well," the captain said, growing uneasy, "we'd like to question him about some mail coach robberies here in the county, and of late I understand that he has been spotted with the murderer Quantrill. You wouldn't happen to be purchasing those revolver caps for him, would you?"

"Why, Captain," Caitlin said and blushed. "I am surprised that you question my word. As I said, these caps are for my Uncle Fitz, bless his soul. If it wasn't for him and his squirrel rifle we would have had many a hungry night. As for my brother, I haven't seen him in more than two weeks. I am sure he is following the dictates of his conscience, just as my other brothers are doing. You know my big brother Frank is with Halleck in St. Louis?"

"No, I did not."

"Captain— What is your name?"

"Blake, ma'am."

"Captain Blake, I am certain that General Halleck would be most displeased to learn that you have accused Frank's only sister of lying and attempting to aid the enemy," Caitlin said. "As everyone knows, my father was a peace Democrat, and he was fully behind the Union of these states."

"That's right," Wilson said.

"I beg your pardon, ma'am," Blake said. "I meant no disrespect."

"I'm sure you didn't," Caitlin said indignantly. "Now, if you will excuse me, I have several other errands to attend to."

She paid for the items and left.

The captain watched her go, and when the door had shut he turned to Wilson and remarked, "She certainly is a little wildcat, isn't she?"

Quantrill and his men had new mounts within a day of the fight at the Tate farm. Some of the horses were stolen and others were supplied by Missourians who saw Quantrill as a hero.

The former schoolmaster regrouped his command in Jackson County and Zachary easily found the location through the network of sympathetic eyes and ears that laced every township along the border. Despite the casualties left behind at the Tate farm, his command continued to grow, and when he lead his men out of Jackson County toward Warrensburg a few days later, Quantrill rode at the head of a column of two hundred riders.

At Warrensburg they hurled themselves against a sixty-man detachment of the Seventh Missouri Cavalry, which had barricaded itself inside the brick Johnson County Courthouse. For all of one day and part of the next Quantrill rushed the fortified position, but could not take it. He finally left the field with nine dead and seventeen wounded, and moodily declared that he would never again assault a brick building.

Returning to Jackson County, Quantrill and his men bivouacked at a farm belonging to a man named Clark and were attacked by the First Missouri Cavalry. Intoxicated as usual by the desperate fight, Quantrill ran repeatedly between the farmhouse and a smokehouse to draw the Yankees' fire while his men potted those foolish enough to expose themselves trying to shoot at the guerrilla leader. Quantrill and his men finally managed to escape into the woods—while farmers with large-caliber rifles kept the Union troops at bay—but they again lost a score of their horses to the enemy. Quantrill ordered his men to disperse to frustrate attempts to follow them, and the column evaporated into the countryside.

Zachary was not given to the camaraderie that marked the personalities of the other riders, and found himself alone at the end of March. It suited his mood. He rode mostly at night, not with any particular goal in mind except to avoid Yankee patrols. Zachary had learned his lessons well with Quantrill, and instead of a single revolver he now carried four Colt navies, two in his belt and two on his saddle, all loaded and ready for action at a moment's notice.

The guerrillas' major advantage over the occupying Union army—besides a vast network of sympathizers and informants—was that they were mounted on the best horses available. With their revolvers, they were capable of laying down a virtual barrage of fire. The regular soldier was typically limited to a rifle that had to be reloaded between shots, wore a uniform that was easily identified as the enemy's, and were little more than human targets placed around strategic points.

So it was that Zachary was in no particular discomfort over his situation as he ranged alone over the countryside, waiting for word that Quantrill's raiders were regrouping. His primary occupation was to find food and shelter, and these were readily offered by sympathetic strangers. He never stayed in one place for more than a day or two before moving, usually in the still of night.

It was late in the afternoon on the first Saturday in April that Zachary found himself in the hayloft of a barn and heard the racket that a squad of six mounted federal soldiers made as they rode into the lot. From a knothole in one of the planks he watched while the farmer, Norman Jones, sauntered out of the house to talk with the young lieutenant who was in charge of the detachment. The night before, Zachary had shared fried chicken with the Jones family at the kitchen table. This morning, Jones acted as if he were hard of hearing and made the lieutenant repeat his orders.

"We're searching for guerrillas," the lieutenant shouted down at Jones, who had a hand cupped theatrically around his ear. The lieutenant wore a full-length dark blue or black cloak and presented a fine, dashing figure on his mount, Zachary thought. "You haven't seen anyone suspicious in the last couple of days, have you?"

Jones innocently shook his head.

"Then you won't mind if we search your house and barn."

"What?"

"I said, we need to search the house and barn."

Zachary smiled as he realized Jones was making the lieutenant shout so as to alert him to the presence of the troops.

"You're welcome to, but be sure to wipe your feet before you go into the house," Jones said, "or Ma will have a fit. Would you like some coffee and a piece of pie?"

"No, sir," the lieutenant said, and motioned two of his men toward the house and directed the other three toward the barn. The men nudged their horses in Zachary's direction.

Zachary was pleased as he shinnied down the ladder into the stall where Raven was waiting. At least he wouldn't have to take on all six of them at once. He threw Raven's saddle over his back, cinched it tight, and quickly put on the bridle and bit. By the time he was finished he could hear the soldiers talking outside the barn door. They were discussing how they should approach the structure, and they decided that two would go in the front while the third remained in back.

By the time the barn door swung open Zachary was in the saddle, with the reins between his teeth and a revolver in each hand. As soon as he saw daylight he dug his heels into Raven's flanks and the horse bolted forward, nearly trampling the soldier who had dismounted to open the door. Zachary shot the other soldier twice in the chest before he could even take his carbine from the saddle ring. He turned Raven and bore down again on the soldier at the door, who was trying to mount his skittish horse.

"Give it up," Zachary said, and the soldier abandoned the horse and ran for the cover of the house. He nudged Raven again and he flew around the side of the barn, and as he rounded the corner he collided with the third soldier, who was racing to help his comrades. Both horses reared in a tangle of reins and hooves and Raven viciously sank his teeth into the other horse. Both Zachary and the Union soldier were thrown on the ground. The soldier had dropped his carbine in the fall, and as he struggled to his feet, he drew his saber from its scabbard. Zachary, who lay on his back but still held one of the guns in his right hand, shot him in the stomach as the soldier held the blade poised above his head. The saber slipped from his fingers as he placed his hands over the wound and fell to his knees.

A rifle sounded from near the house and splintered the side of the barn near Zachary's shoulder as he snatched up his other revolver and scrambled to the back of the barn for protection. Raven was trailing his reins in the lot, and peering around the corner Zachary saw one of the soldiers rise up over the stone fence near the house and level his rifle at the horse. Zachary fired twice and the soldier abandoned the target and ducked back under the protection of the fence.

Zachary put his fingers in his mouth and whistled and Raven picked up his ears and then trotted over to the back of the barn. Zachary shot twice again to keep the soldiers behind the fence. When Raven came within reach he swung into the saddle and started to head for the wood line, then reconsidered because he didn't want to present his back as a target for the soldiers' carbines. He reined the horse to a stop. He drank in the adrenaline rush of battle. He felt *alive* for the first time since . . . Well, since they had rushed the barricades at Warrensburg. He grinned, turned Raven, and reached full gallop by the time he came around the corner of the barn. He bore down on the stone fence where he knew at least one of the soldiers hid. As Raven jumped over the fence he gave a rebel yell and fired both pistols. One of the balls shattered a trooper's shoulder. Then he brought Raven up hard against the lieutenant and leveled both pistols at his head.

"You men throw down your arms, unless you want one dead officer," Zachary said.

The lieutenant closed his eyes and dropped his revolver. His blond hair was cut short and his mustache was as fine as goose down. His cheeks were flushed with embarrassment.

The soldier with the shoulder wound made no attempt to recover his rifle, but the other held his in both hands, unsure of what to do, the barrel wavering.

"Lieutenant?" he asked.

"Kill him," the lieutenant said.

"If that's the way you want it," Zachary said, and cocked the pistol.

"Wait," the soldier said. "I give." He let his rifle drop to the ground.

"You shouldn't have done that, soldier," the lieutenant said. "Now he's going to kill all of us. You could have at least saved yourself."

"I'm not going to kill you," Zachary said. "You two, move over here where I can see you, and put your hands behind your head. Yes, like so. You ain't Kansans, are you?"

"No," the lieutenant said. "We're from the First Iowa."

"I reckon I can spare you, as long as you accept field paroles. Otherwise, if you stuck up for the Union, I'd have to kill you."

Zachary carefully dismounted, keeping one of the revolvers pointing at the lieutenant. He stooped down and retrieved the .44-caliber revolver from the dirt and slipped it into the nearer of Raven's saddlebags. Then he took the lieutenant's hat and placed it on the ground, upside down.

"I want you to take all of your money and put it in that hat," Zachary said. "Watches, too, if you got 'em, and tobacco."

"This is outrageous," the lieutenant said.

"Look, I'm going to give you a field parole and let you tend to your dead and wounded right soon. Otherwise, I have to shoot you. I think it's only fair, because I would have hung if *you* had captured *me*. I think it's more than fair, don't you?"

"Well," the lieutenant said. "It's not exactly . . . well, yes, I guess it is rather fair, considering. Do you think it's fair, men?"

"Oh, yes," the formerly indecisive soldier answered.

The lieutenant emptied the contents of his pockets into his own hat, and the wounded soldier struggled to get his items out of his pockets. The other soldier quickly emptied everything he had into the hat, and then tugged at the wedding band on his left hand.

"No," Zachary said. "Keep that. Some things are sacred even in war."

"Thank you."

Zachary picked up the hat and dumped the contents into the

other saddlebag. Then he asked for the lieutenant's saber, and the young man offered it, hilt first. Zachary slipped the blade under his belt.

"I want your cloak, too."

"I beg your pardon, sir?"

Zachary smiled.

"Your cloak, I fancy it."

"My mother gave it to me," the man said lamely as he slipped the cloak from his shoulders. "Nights are damned cold here on the frontier, even in spring." It was indeed black, with a black satin lining. Zachary draped the garment over his arm and swung back into Raven's saddle.

"Begging the lieutenant's pardon," the married soldier said, "but it weren't *proper* military issue."

"That will be enough, Harris."

"Yes, sir."

"Raise your right hands," Zachary said. "That's right, raise 'em up. Now, do you promise to . . . to lay down your guns and never to take them up again against the Confederate States of America?"

They promised, shifting uncomfortably and shuffling their feet. Harris smiled.

"You have to mean it," Zachary admonished.

"We swear it," Harris said.

"Good enough," Zachary said. "Now, I want you to understand that you surprised me while I was stealing this man's horse from his barn. He's a good-for-nothing Yankee-loving reptile, and I have him marked."

Jones, who was standing in his front door watching, called out: "That's my horse!"

"Shut up, you," Zachary replied, and turned Raven toward the road. The sun was almost down and threw long shadows from the hedgerow across Zachary's path.

"Who are you?" the lieutenant called boldly.

"Hell, don't you know?" He grinned. "I'm the dark rider. There's them that say I'm a ghost, that I can't be killed, and there's others that claim I'm the devil himself. You can make up your own mind."

He touched his heels to Raven's flanks. He could scarcely contain his mirth. He could already imagine himself relating the story to Bill Quantrill and having a good laugh over it.

Two weeks to the night after Caitlin had tended his wounds and Sarah had mended his shirt, Zachary returned to the Little Shannon Valley at about midnight and rode to the lonely family plot on the side of the hill. He dismounted and sat for some time on his heels between the graves of his father and mother, and he looked longingly at the farmhouse. A single lantern glowed in the kitchen window. Then he went over to the oak tree and reached inside the blackened trunk. His hand found a grain sack and he pulled it out.

There were two tins of percussion caps, some tobacco, some cornbread and a bit of ham wrapped in a piece of oilcloth, and a penciled note.

Dearest Zachary,

I pray you are well. Please be careful. The Yankees have a warrant with your name on it and they will hang you if they catch you. Please think about leaving for a spell. Don't worry about us—the most important thing is that you are safe. I am fine and so are the others. I love you and miss you terribly.

Sarah

Zachary smiled. How would they survive without the little bit of money he gave them now and again? He took the things out of the grain sack and replaced them with a handful of greenbacks, then put the sack back into the tree trunk. He pulled his cloak around his shoulders and climbed back into the saddle.

19

August 1862

QUANTRILL, wearing his red battle shirt, was flanked by George Todd on one side and Zachary Fenn on the other as he led the column over the prairie toward Independence. George Todd was smoking a cigar and he wore his slouch hat at a decidedly rakish angle. Zachary wore no hat, and his hair, which had gone uncut in the last several months, fell in curls to his shoulders. He was wearing the black cloak he had appropriated from the young lieutenant, and the brass trigger guards of his matched pair of Colt revolvers gleamed beneath it.

Zachary, whose audacity in battle nearly matched his leader's, had become one of Quantrill's most valued—if not trusted—men. Zachary had been at his side when they looted the steamboat *Little Blue* at Sibley and later, when they fought the First Missouri and First Iowa at the Sears farm, near Pleasant Hill, it was Zachary who rode through a Union fusillade to pick up Quantrill after a horse was shot out from beneath him.

There was nothing that Bill Quantrill admired more than dash, and if Zachary Fenn disappeared for a few days or a week at a time, that was his business. Most of the boys slipped away now and again to see their families or sweethearts, and they asked for little enough in return.

In his last visit to the blackened stump near the graves of his parents, Zachary had left twenty dollars in gold and a hastily scrawled note asking for Sarah to meet him at their intended homestead along the banks of Sugar Creek during the next full moon. Days in the bush were sometimes hard to reckon and it would be easier to watch the moon, which was now three-quarters full.

Zachary touched his breast pocket as he thought of Sarah, for that was where he kept her most recent note. Quantrill had advised him to rid himself of any documents which would identify him or implicate his family, against the possibility that he would be killed or captured, but Zachary could not bring himself to discard the notes. Their presence seemed to bring her nearer, somehow. Besides, he did not believe there was a corner he *couldn't* fight out of.

The column was passing over the Doc Lee prairie toward the Confederate recruiting headquarters that Colonel Upton Hays had established brazenly close to the Union garrison at Independence. The Confederate battle flag that flew on the tall staff in the center of the camp could be seen quite clearly from Union Lieutenant Colonel James T. Buel's headquarters in the stone bank building, just off the Independence square. If Buel were concerned about the Confederate presence, he did not betray it; not only had he failed to send out any patrols in the past few days, but the three hundred men in his command were located in an appallingly indefensible tent camp a half a mile away from headquarters. Consequently, Buel did not know that several companies of Confederate cavalry, both regular and partisan, were massing on the prairie. Recruiting had been excellent and, between them, Hays and Quantrill commanded more than three hundred and fifty men. In addition, there were five companies of regular cavalry that had followed the Missouri River north to assist in the assault upon Independence.

As they entered camp, Quantrill stood in the saddle and craned his neck behind him. With a motion of his arm he directed Bill Haller and William Gregg to dismount and picket the horses. Quantrill rode to Upton's tent before dismounting, and he gave his reins over to Zachary. The flaps of the tent were open and Colonel Hays, who had been leaning over a desk studying a map of the area, strode out and warmly shook Quantrill's hand.

"How are you, Captain?" Hays asked.

"Passable," Quantrill answered. "I'll be better when I have Buel in my sights."

Hays poured him a shot of whiskey, and after Quantrill had cut the dust from his throat, they sat in field chairs inside the tent and discussed the battle plan.

"I want your column to attack Buel's headquarters," Hays said. "Your men are quick and they are familiar with street fighting, and we must be sure to cut Buel off from his troops first thing. Besides, just the sound of your name ought to send a few shivers down his spine."

Quantrill smiled vainly.

"Here's the situation. Buel and his staff are located in the Southern Bank building, a block off the square here," he said, and pointed to the map. "A guard company is stationed across the street, and the provost marshal's office is located in the jail. In addition, there are guard posts at the end of each of these streets. An hour before dawn tomorrow, you and your men are to sweep down on the headquarters and kill, or at least capture, Buel."

"What is the guard company's strength?" Quantrill asked.

"Fifty to sixty men."

The guerrilla chief nodded and placed his hands behind his head. "This ought to be easier than shooting ducks on a pond," Quantrill said.

At 4:30 the next morning Quantrill and his column were again in the saddle and ready for battle. They had slipped quietly into Independence while the town slept and were poised in the darkness just three blocks from the Union headquarters. They would enter the square in one group and then divide into three detachments. Todd was to engage the guard company, Gregg was to seize the provost marshal's office and release the prisoners, and Quantrill himself would assault the bank building.

Quantrill fired a match and lit a cigar before ordering the final charge. A few paces behind, Zachary Fenn shifted anxiously in the saddle, more from excitement than fear. His revolvers were loaded and capped and Raven's tack had been carefully soaped and the rings greased with lard. Zachary nudged Raven forward to pull alongside Quantrill.

"Have another cigar, Bill?"

Quantrill took one from his shirt pocket and handed it over, then held the match while Zachary sucked fire into it. The smoke burned Zachary's throat and lungs but seemed to heighten his excitement.

"We must fight like demons," Quantrill said in a low voice. "If we're captured they will shoot us on the spot, as they did Porter's men. No quarter."

Zachary nodded.

Quantrill turned, raised his right hand above his head, and brought it down sharply. The column surged forward, the shod hooves of the horses making a fearful racket and throwing sparks from the roadway. The surprised guards at the end of Spring Street were trod under amid popping revolvers and Rebel yells. Then the column split into three.

Zachary was hard on Quantrill's flank as they bore down on the bank building. A sentry stationed at the entrance to the bank had witnessed the riders overrun at the post at the end of the street and he dashed for the guard company across the street, shouting the alarm. The guerrillas swarmed in front of the bank, shooting out windows, but before they could dismount and rush the front door they were answered by a volley of rifle fire from across the street. A handful of the guerrillas fell from their horses as the group broke for cover.

Quantrill cursed heavily and made for the safety of the street corner. They had not been quick enough to cut the guard company away from Buel. With the way cleared, the half-dressed company dashed across the street in squads and quickly began to barricade themselves in the bank building.

Meanwhile, the jail was taken easily. The provost guard broke and ran in the direction of Kansas City on foot while Gregg freed the prisoners. Simultaneously a half mile away, Buel's main force was under attack by the Confederate regulars, and after a brief fight most of them fled as well.

Quantrill directed his men to dismount and take up positions along storefronts and wagons and begin a sniping operation against the headquarters. They exchanged shots for the next three hours without strategically changing the situation, and finally Quantrill ordered firing ceased.

"Damned stone building," he said. "We're going to have to try something a little different here. It looks like we're going to have to smoke this skunk out. If the sonuvabitch doesn't want to surrender, he can roast."

Quantrill ordered Zachary to round up a squad of men to set fire to the wooden store building next door to the bank. The sun was well into the sky and it was becoming warm, so Zachary dropped his cloak and tapped the three men closest to him. The four inched their way along the storefronts, keeping out of sight of the Union snipers in the bank building, and broke through the front windows of the land office. They smashed coal oil lamps over the walls and counters and set a match to the office. As they jumped back through the window to make a dash to the safety of their lines, Zachary's shirt caught on one of the ragged shards of glass and ripped. The notes from Sarah spilled out onto the sidewalk, and he groped to gather them up. A sniper in the top window of the bank building spotted Zachary on his hands and knees on the sidewalk and sent down a round, but because of the acute angle the shot went high and splattered the bricks near Zachary's hand. Zachary ran off, clutching the notes to his chest.

Thirty minutes later, with fire consuming the building next door and smoke pouring heavily into the bank building, a white flag appeared in an upper window. Buel arranged a surrender to the Confederate regulars—who had by now thoroughly finished routing the tent camp—on the condition that he and his men wouldn't be turned over to Quantrill.

Fearing quick retaliation by Union forces at Kansas City and elsewhere, Quantrill gathered his force that afternoon and rode for their secret camp at the Morgan Walker farm in Jackson County. The guerrillas had paid heavily for their victory at Independence, leaving nearly forty of their number dead, mostly from the first clash with the guard company. But the defeat of a major federal military installation struck new fear in the Yankees. For Quantrill, the engagement carried an even more shining dividend—his company was sanctioned under the Partisan Ranger Act by the Confederate command and Quantrill himself received a field commission as captain.

The Union did mount an offensive to cut off the Rebel force, but lacked the speed which Quantrill had feared. General Blunt was dispatched from Fort Scott at the head of two thousand infantry, but they traveled at a snail's pace because Blunt employed prairie schooners drawn by mules to move his command. Major Emory Foster and eight hundred men and two cannon were put on the trail from Lexington, and the First Iowa under General Warren was mounted in Clinton, but they failed to coordinate the envisioned net that would trap the Rebels. Instead, on the morning of August 16, Foster's bivouac at Lone Jack was encircled by two thousand Missouri guerrillas and, after a bloody house-to-house fight, surrendered. Although the Union authorities blamed the defeat on Quantrill, he in fact had returned to quiet Independence with most of his command to pick up supplies that had been left behind.

"Damn, Captain Quantrill," Zachary said after reading the papers a few days after the Lone Jack fight, "the Yankees are so scared of you that they're seeing your shadow everywhere."

The night was still and the full moon was high among the stars as Zachary waited in the stand of trees on the side of the hill near Sugar Creek. He had shaved and combed his long hair and beaten the dust out of his clothes, and he sat on a rough army blanket spread beneath the bows of an elm. On a tin plate in the center of the blanket was a wedge of cheese and a loaf of hard bread that he had taken from camp, and a battered old book he had carried in his saddlebags for many months. He reckoned by the stars that it was long past midnight and he dejectedly began to put these things away when he heard the sound of hooves.

He stood still for a moment, his hand resting on the butt of his revolver, and then he caught a wisp of white moving through the trees. He spoke and in a moment Sarah was in his arms.

"I had almost forgotten how good you smell," he said, caressing the girl's cheek. "I love you."

"Oh, Zachary," she said, "I love you too, and I have been so lonely for you for so very long. I'm sorry I'm late. It was hard to find my way in the dark."

He kissed her and then held her tightly. She closed her eyes and laid her head against his chest. Their embrace continued for several long minutes, with neither of them speaking, and then Sarah drew back from him. Her eyes gleamed in the moonlight.

"I was afraid I would never see you again," she said. Then she carefully undid the buttons of her blouse, took Zachary's rough hand, and placed it between her breasts.

"Do you feel my heart?"

"Yes."

Still clasping his hand to her, she reached out with her other hand and worked it through the folds of his shirt until it rested on his bare chest.

"There," she said. "I feel yours. Our hearts beat as one. They always will, no matter how far you may range from me. I want you to make love to me, Zachary, because I don't know how long it will be before I see you again . . . or *if* I ever see you again."

He cupped his hands around her and kissed her, and they fell to the blanket together. He knocked aside the plate of food and undressed her, and she slipped his shirt over his head. Her body shone like ivory in the moonlight, and he touched her gently as if for fear she might break.

"I have never seen anything more beautiful than you are right now," he said. "There is nothing more important to me than you, and when this war is over we will make a life together, here on this land. And we will have lots of children."

"Yes," Sarah said, and drew him down to her.

For the next few hours the war seemed very far away.

20

May 1863

FITZ HAD BEEN WORKING a small patch of turnips and he leaned on his hoe while he watched the soldiers turn into the road that led up the hill to the house. There were seven troopers, with an officer in the lead, and a wagon was trailing behind. As they grew closer he relaxed somewhat as he saw they were regular army, not Jayhawkers. The officer reined his horse to a stop and touched the brim of his hat.

"Sir, I understand that you are Zachary Fenn's uncle."

"I am," Fitz said.

"I am Captain Jonas Blake and I carry an arrest warrant for your nephew. He is charged with murder, robbery, and arson. Is he here?"

"No."

"Do you know where he is?"

"I haven't seen Zachary in a month of Sundays," Fitz said. "And if I did know where he was, I wouldn't tell."

"I'm sure you wouldn't," Blake said. "We will be required to search your property. Be kind enough to remain outside while we do."

"Search away," Fitz said, "but you'd better knock first, because there's three women and a child in that house. You'll scare the daylights out of them if you barge in. You ain't going to burn us out, are you?"

"No, sir. We're not Kansans." Blake dismounted and directed three of the soldiers to search the barn while he led the others toward the house. He strode up to the front door and rapped loudly, then stepped to one side. After a few moments Caitlin opened the door.

"Captain," she said. "Why are you standing over there?"

"I'm sorry, miss, but some folks tend to answer a knock with a shotgun blast," he said. "I've explained to your uncle that we have an arrest warrant for Zachary and that we are here to search the property. Would you call the others, and please step outside while we conduct our search."

"I'm afraid your manners have not improved since our last meeting," Caitlin said.

"It is hard to be a gentleman in these times," he said. "I am surprised you remember that day in Harrisonville, our paths crossed so briefly."

"It was your rudeness that struck my memory," she said, and turned to get the others.

Blake smiled. In other circumstances, he might be here courting this strong-willed girl instead of enforcing orders that he found personally repugnant.

Caitlin reappeared, with Sarah and Jenny in tow. Jenny was carrying nineteen-month-old Little Frank in her arms, and at the sight of the man in officer's uniform the child tugged at his mother's dress.

"No, sugar, that's not Papa," Jenny said. "Papa's still in St. Louis."

Fitz stood with the women while the soldiers searched the house from the top down to the cellar. Soon the soldiers returned from the barn and reported that it was empty also.

"Check the well," Blake ordered.

Two of the men held another by his heels and lowered him partially into the well.

"Empty, sir," the soldiers called.

"I see," Blake said. "Which one of you women is Sarah Drake?"

"I am," Sarah said. "Why?"

Blake flushed.

"This is most unpleasant," he said apologetically. "I have orders here from General Ewing in Kansas City . . ."

"You mean Lane's yellow dog, Tom Ewing?" Fitz asked. "Ewing doesn't make water without checking with Jim Lane to see if it's allowed. Sorry, girls."

Sarah began to shake.

"What manner of orders, Captain Blake?" Caitlin asked, and she put a hand on Sarah's arm.

"You are Zachary's fiancée?" Blake asked.

"What orders?" Caitlin repeated.

"Orders to arrest her for giving aid and comfort to Zachary Fenn. General Ewing has ordered that many wives and girlfriends of the more . . . noteworthy members of Quantrill's band be confined for the duration."

"You must be mistaken," Caitlin said. "It is true that Sarah and Zachary are sweethearts, but this girl is a Quaker. War is against her religion and she takes neither side."

"I'm sorry, but there is evidence against her."

"What evidence?"

"I am really not authorized to discuss it, but I will tell you so that things may be clear between us. A note from Sarah advising Zachary that Union officers were inquiring about his activities was found on the street outside Buel's headquarters. We have been in possession of this for some time, and Quantrill's depredations no longer make it possible for us to ignore it. I am afraid she will have to come with us."

"Here, now," Fitz said, stepping between Blake and the girls. "I cannot let you do this. Get off of our property this instant, or you and I will have a right smart go-round."

"For your sake, I will pretend that I did not hear that," Blake said.

Caitlin placed a hand on Fitz's shoulder.

"Please, Uncle," she said. "It will do us no good for you to be hauled off to prison as well. You must stay here and watch over Jenny and Little Frank."

"But, Cait—"

"Shush," she said. "It will be all right."

"Can I get my things?" Sarah asked, fighting back tears.

"Yes, but a soldier must accompany you."

"Wait," Caitlin said. "You had better send a soldier with me to get my things as well, because I am going with her."

"I'm sorry, but that's impossible."

"Why is it impossible?" Caitlin asked. "If you take her, you must take me as well. It is that simple. Or are you going to claim to be too much of a gentleman?"

"No, miss," he said. "We don't have a warrant for you."

"Well, I am ready to make a confession. These soldiers here are witnesses—"

"Cait," Fitz said. "Don't."

"I was the one who stitched Zachary up when he was wounded and gave him food and hid him and I purchased material for him with money that I presume was stolen from your troops," Caitlin said. "You were absolutely correct the day you questioned me in Harrisonville. I was buying percussion caps for Zachary, and you must take me instead. Sarah did nothing except write him a few notes and express concern for his safety."

Blake ran a hand over his face.

"Why are you doing this?" he asked.

Caitlin faltered for a moment. She looked at the ground, then at Sarah.

"I'm doing this because they love each other," Caitlin said, "and they deserve to be together." Then she added, very low: "And I have no one." She wiped a tear from her face and then stood straight.

"Captain, you cannot allow this to happen," Jenny said. "This woman's brother—my *husband*—is a comrade in arms. He is an adjutant in St. Louis. Surely that must carry some meaning?"

"I wish there was some other way," Blake said. "I cannot release Sarah and now I must take Miss Fenn in as well. Men, go with them and allow them to pack one grip each."

Sarah held her hands folded over her stomach and she leaned heavily against Caitlin.

"I haven't been feeling well lately," she said. "I think I'm going to be ill."

Caitlin helped her inside, and they were followed by the soldiers.

"When will be their trial?" Jenny asked.

"I'm sorry," Blake answered. "Missouri is under martial law and constitutional rights have been suspended. There will be no trial. They will be held for the duration or until—"

"Until what?"

"Until Zachary is dead."

"My God, this can't be happening," Jenny cried. "These people helped a runaway slave escape to Kansas before the war, and Frank and I both fought strongly for the abolitionist cause. And these girls, these *children* you are taking away, have been models of love and compassion. Has the world gone mad?"

"I'm afraid it has, ma'am," Blake said.

"But what can we do?"

"Pray for them," Blake said. "I am truly sorry. I wish that our commanders had half the sand that your sister-in-law displayed today. I hope that one day you may find it in your heart to forgive us, for I am convinced we know not what we do. But this is war, and we are soldiers, and we have our orders."

"I wish to God that you had a heart instead," Jenny said.

"We ought to hit Lawrence," Quantrill said, standing over the maps and jabbing his finger at Douglas County for emphasis. "Burn it to the ground, just like Lane did to Osceola. Desperate times call for desperate measures."

His lieutenants—George Todd, Bill Haller, and William Gregg —were sitting in chairs around the table in the dining room of the Morgan Walker home in Jackson County. Quantrill had taken the band south to Arkansas to winter with Shelby's brigade, and in early May they had worked their way back up the border. They were under orders to keep the Union forces occupied while Sterling Price mounted an invasion of Missouri from the southeast. Within days of returning to their old haunts they were burning bridges, pulling down telegraph wires, playing havoc with the mails, and assaulting steamboats. But Quantrill wanted more, and for months he had been arguing for an attack on Lawrence. News from Lawrence still attracted national attention—even though there still weren't more than three thousand souls living there— and Quantrill felt a blow at the free state capital would prove to be a symbolic victory for the Rebels. His men, however, were reluctant to venture forty miles into Kansas and fight the Jayhawkers on their own soil.

"I don't know, Bill," Todd said. "I feel more comfortable being close to home, where we know folks, and where I feel like we're doing some good. Hitting Lawrence would just make it double hot for us here."

"I agree with George," Haller said. "It's one thing to jump across the line to Aubrey, but it's another to make for Lawrence. There's closer and better targets for us."

"But Lawrence is the head of the snake," Quantrill said. "If we can capture Lane, we can put an end to his waltzing over the line and roasting our towns when he feels like it."

"I would rather catch Lane's Brigade on our side of the border," Gregg said, "and whip him in a head-to-head fight. That would make the Redlegs think twice before crossing the line."

Quantrill shook his head.

"What's it going to take for you boys to realize that we need to wipe out Lane where he lives?" he asked. "Another Osceola? He wiped that town clean off the map. By the time he burns another town it will be too late, we will have lost too much. All of you have families that have suffered because of Lane, or Jennison, or Montgomery. How much more suffering is it going to take?"

"I'm sorry, Bill," Todd said. "I'll talk it over with the boys in my outfit, but I don't think they're going to like it any better than I do."

"You'll see," Quantrill said. "Lane is not finished yet. Before this is all over you'll be begging me to take you over to Lawrence to settle the score."

Zachary was sitting on a stump, eating an apple, and reading from a book of poetry he had found in a deserted farmhouse during their stay in Arkansas. It was the middle of the afternoon and the raiders were idle as Quantrill met with his lieutenants in the big house by the road. Some of them were playing cards and others were drinking, but Zachary hadn't taken a shine to either of those pastimes. Frank James was a reader as well, and they often traded books and talked about things they'd read. Frank was particularly taken with Shakespeare, but the language was too difficult for Zachary. He was reading poetry by a man named Whitman and it was much easier to understand.

A scrawny figure in a greasy buckskin jacket walked into the middle of the camp. He had long hair and a beard and he walked unsteadily, as if he were very sick or very tired. Zachary reckoned him for another refugee that had been burned out of his home, and that the pickets had let come in to beg food to take back to his family. He didn't give the character another thought until he came to stand in front of him.

"Zachary?" the man asked.

He looked up from his book and his jaw dropped a notch when

he recognized his brother beneath the beard and the hair. His face was sunburned and leathery, and he was pitifully thin.

"Damn, Patrick, is that really you?"

"I've come back," Patrick said, and stuck out his hand.

Zachary stood and grasped the hand in both of his, then put his arm around his brother's shoulder and gave him a shake. Patrick was somewhat embarrassed because he and Zachary had never been close, and it had been unusual for them even to touch.

"How was the wilderness?"

"It was wild, all right," Patrick said with a sheepish grin. "I nearly starved to death on the Solomon and the Indians damn near scalped me out in Colorado. The trapping was miserable and I lost my gun to a thieving mule skinner, and in the end I reckoned the war couldn't be no worse than what I had already been through, so I shagged for home."

"So you've been to the Little Shannon Valley?" Zachary asked. "I haven't been back since before Colonel Quantrill took us to Arkansas last year. How is everybody? Did you see Sarah? What about Jenny and Little Frank?"

"Yeah, I've been to the farm," Patrick said. "Fitz told me where to find you. Zach, I don't know how to tell you this except to just say it. The Yankees have arrested Caitlin and Sarah and have locked them up in prison at Kansas City."

"Arrested them?" Zachary asked, bewildered. "What for?"

"For helping you," Patrick said. "For buying percussion caps and passing you notes and such. Fitz sent me to tell you about it. He's madder than a hornet and he swears he'll kill the next Yankee that sets foot on the farm."

Zachary swallowed hard and looked away from Patrick for a moment. What a fool he had been to have come back to the farm even once.

"I'll turn myself in," Zachary said.

"You cannot," Patrick said. "They have a warrant for your arrest and they will hang you if they catch you. The girls don't want you dead, Zach, and neither do I."

Zachary was silent for a moment. He felt as if the world were closing in on him.

"Tell Fitz that I'll do anything to get them out."

"I ain't going back," Patrick said. "I've come to join with you, Zach. I didn't want any part of this war, but they've forced it upon me. I cannot stand by and let them ruin our family without doing something about it. Let me ride with you, Zach."

"You know what they do to guerrillas."

"I know what they did to our sister and to your Sarah. It ain't civilized for them to be putting our women in jail. I know you and Colonel Quantrill ain't never touched one of their women, and wouldn't, not for anything. It ain't right what they done, and I am here to make them pay."

"I'd be proud to have you ride with me," Zachary said. "Get your horse and tie him up with Raven over there, then we'll get you some mess. You look like you're half starved."

"I don't have a horse. Mine died, and the Jayhawkers have taken them all from the farm."

"We'll get you a horse," Zachary said. "And a gun or two. The Yankees have been right nice about letting us borrow what we need from them."

"Zach," Patrick said, "I know I haven't been solid with you, nor the rest of the family neither. But I've changed. The wilderness gave me plenty of time to think, and I thought right hard about all of us, and I reckon there are some things a man just has to fight for."

21

August 1863

I T WAS DUSK and the column moved like a long black snake across the countryside toward Kansas. Quantrill's command of three hundred fifty riders had been joined by one hundred regular Confederate troops under the command of Colonel John D. Holt, who was returning from a recruiting mission in northern Missouri. They crossed the border into Johnson County and two companies of Union soldiers rode out from the post at Aubrey to challenge them, but stopped short when they saw the size of the Rebel force. Quantrill, riding at the head of the column, gave the order which was passed down the line: "Do not fire unless fired upon."

Zachary Fenn looked with hatred upon the bluecoats across the prairie, and his rage swelled to consume him. He closed his eyes and held tight onto the saddle horn, and the crimson scars on both of his forearms ached anew. In his mind he relived the moment, a week before, when it seemed all that he held dear in life had been taken from him. . . .

The afternoon had been hot and not a breath of wind stirred in the trees along the river. Raven picked his way down the bank and walked out into the riverbed, and Zachary let him stand belly-deep in the cold, clear water. Zachary leaned down and submerged his kerchief and then placed it over the back of his neck, letting the icy rivulets run down his back.

The other raiders came down the bank also, dipping their canteens and letting their horses drink their fill. Cole Younger rode out into the stream, scooped up a hatful of water, and dashed it over his head.

"Damn, but that feels good," Cole said. "Burning bridges is hot work. Did you see those guards leave their lunch and hightail it for cover when we came out of the tree line?"

Zachary had smiled, for perhaps the last time. The Yankees had given up the bridge without firing a shot. They would rebuild it in a week or two, and then Quantrill and the boys would return to burn it again.

All summer the guerrillas had been on the move, disrupting lines of supply and communication for miles on both sides of the border. Apart from an occasional skirmish, they had met little resistance.

Suddenly a rider approached from the woods. He flung his horse down the bank and nearly tumbled from the saddle as his mount lost its footing, sending mud and stones skittering into the water. Quantrill had dismounted and was walking along the edge of a broad sandbar, occasionally picking up a flat stone and skipping it across the water. Cole and Zachary watched as the rider galloped across through the shallow water toward Quantrill, rainbows dancing in the spray from the hooves.

"Here, now," Quantrill said, shielding his face from the water as the rider drew up. "What the hell is wrong?"

"Colonel Quantrill, I've brought news from Kansas City," the boy said, dropping from the saddle and wading onto the sandbar. "My name is Nathan Harris. I'm John and Thomas Harris's little brother."

"Yes," Quantrill said. "They are good men. What news?"

"It just happened this morning," he said. "I came as fast—"

"What *news?*" Quantrill barked.

Zachary had jumped down from Raven and was among the other guerrillas forming a knot around Quantrill and the boy. Any news from Kansas City surely had to be bad news.

"Me and Ma went to see my sister at the old three-story brick building on Grand Avenue, the one where they have kept the women prisoners," the boy said, struggling for breath. "It collapsed. Five or six of the girls are dead and there are some who are very badly hurt. It's been propped up for some time with girders underneath it, and there were some in the crowd that said Tom Ewing had the girders removed to cause it to fall down. Ma told me to go find you and tell you about it just as quick as I could."

"Ewing," Quantrill said with contempt. "I'll bet Lane's behind this."

"Who was killed?" Cole Younger asked.

"Christie Kerr," the boy said. "Josephine Anderson, Sue Vandiver, Armena Giley."

Bill Anderson fell to his knees on the sandbar. He began to wail and pull fistfuls of his long black hair from his head and cry over his sister, Josephine. Anderson was a steadfast but undistinguished rider who had come from Council Grove, Kansas, to join Quantrill after his father was killed by Jayhawkers.

"That was only four," Cole asked. "Slow down and think. Who else?"

The boy nodded and caught his breath. The only sound from among the raiders as they waited on the boy was Bill Anderson's anguished crying.

"Sarah Blake," the boy said.

Zachary's blood ran suddenly as cold as the river water.

"Blake," Zachary said. "Are you sure?"

"Yes," the boy said. "No. Wait. It was Sarah Drake, not Blake. That's it. Crushed to death. And among the worst injured were Mary Anderson, Martha Munday, Cait Fenn, and my sister, Nannie."

"My God," Quantrill said. "Now they are killing our women."

Zachary stood very still. Cole Younger put an arm around his shoulders and awkwardly gave him a shake.

"Are you with us, hoss?" Cole asked.

Zachary tried to speak, but couldn't. Everything—the sky, the river, the trees—seemed pointless, empty, dead. Two of the raiders had grabbed Anderson and pinned his arms to his sides to keep him from hurting himself further.

"Zach, I'm real sorry," Cole said.

"It should have been me," Zachary said, finally, blinking back the tears. "I should have turned myself in, should have let them hang me. God, if I could only go back. I promised I'd *protect* her. I *promised*. Now they've done killed her."

Cole looked at the tops of his boots, not knowing what to say.

"Do you know how bad Caitlin's hurt?" Zachary asked the boy.

"I believe she got her leg crushed, but I'm not sure how bad off she is," he said. "Everything was real confusing, and they wouldn't let us get close."

"Do me a favor," Zachary told Cole. "Go find Patrick and tell him what happened. Tell him Caitlin's hurt but we don't know how bad. Take care of my horse for me. I need to be alone a spell."

Cole nodded and walked off. The raiders were milling about, unusually quiet for such a rough bunch of men, until George Todd spoke up.

"Colonel," Todd said, "I think it's about time we held a war council and decided what to do about this. Maybe you were right all along. Maybe we should have taken Lawrence to the ground a long time ago."

Zachary walked alone down the riverbank, and when he was out of sight of the others he sank to his knees in the sand near the bows of a willow tree. Slowly he pulled one of the Colt navies out of his belt, looked it over as if for the first time, and placed the barrel in his mouth. It tasted of oil and gunpowder. He put his thumb in the trigger guard and used his forefinger to draw the hammer back. The cylinder spun as the action locked in place. The hammer was poised to fall on a bright copper percussion cap, twenty grains of powder, and a leaden ball. He tightened his grip on the gun as he imagined the ball carrying the back of his head away. Then he stopped. His brother Patrick would find him, pick up the pieces of his shattered skull and bury him, and have to tell Caitlin and the others what had happened. His hand went slack and the gun dropped into the sand.

Misery washed over him and the tears brimmed over and spilled down his cheeks, blurring his vision and dimming the world. It felt like there was a hole inside him, as if his heart had been ripped beating from his chest. He realized that Sarah's heart had ceased to beat at all and the darkness engulfed him. A hate as seamless and complete as anything he had ever known consumed him. If he were to live, he thought, then let his hate and desire for revenge be as perfect as his love for Sarah had been.

He opened his eyes and drew the knife from his belt. He pulled back the sleeve from his left forearm and cut four diagonal slashes in the taut skin over the muscle. The pain was keen and drew him back into the world. He switched the knife to his other hand, pulled back the sleeve from his right forearm, and made four matching cuts there as well. The blood ran down his arms and spilled onto the ground. As the Yankees had made him bleed, had taken his very life, he would take from them. He would become the maker of widows, the father of orphans, the very instrument of the grim angel of death. Hell itself would reign on earth.

Zachary rubbed the angry scars on his left forearm as the column pressed on through the growing darkness. If the raiders had any doubts about Ewing's intention to utterly destroy their families, it was dispelled when Order Number Ten was issued on the heels of the prison collapse in Kansas City. Ewing had ordered that the wives and children of known guerrillas be removed by force from their homes and taken out of the state to points south. When Quantrill gathered the raiders together on the Blackwater River for the war council, the decision to strike Lawrence was largely theirs.

Some weeks before, Quantrill had sent a spy, Fletcher Taylor, into Lawrence. Taylor, disguised as a horse trader, had checked in at the Eldridge Hotel and even had dinner in the hotel dining room with the hated Jim Lane. Fletcher reported back that, fearing attack, the authorities had posted guards at every entrance to the city and cannon had been rolled onto Massachusetts Street. But the Union troops had been called out of Lawrence to strengthen positions on the border, and the city mayor had ordered that all small arms—even those for the few recruits that were left to guard the city—be locked up in the city armory. There was a garrison stationed across the Kansas River, but a bridge across the river still was under construction and the troops could be easily cut off by securing the ferry landing. In addition, there were still no railways or telegraphs that could be used to alert the town of Quantrill's advance, or to summon troops once the attack began. Lawrence, Taylor reported, was all but defenseless. The most hazardous part of the raid, he said, was the journey to and from Lawrence, with Yankee detachments to be expected at every town.

Taylor had made maps of the city, pinpointing the location of the homes of the staunchest Union supporters and Quantrill had ordered copies made and distributed to the men. The maps comprised a death list, but the location of the prize that Quantrill sought most was missing; Jim Lane had moved and built a new home, and Fletcher was unsure of the location.

Because of the uncertain nature of the mission, and the possibility that at any time they might be cut off and wiped out by superior Union forces, Quantrill made it clear that no raider would be censured for refusing to participate. When the final count was made, two hundred ninety-four guerrillas from Quantrill's command and other bands had volunteered. In addition, there were Holt's hundred recruits, and fifty more guerrillas picked up along the way in Cass County. All told, Quantrill's force was nearly four hundred fifty strong.

As the full moon sank in the sky, the dark column passed at a trot through Gardner, along the old Sante Fe Trail, then pressed on to Hesper, ten miles southeast of Lawrence. They crossed the Wakarusa River at Blue Jacket's Crossing. Dawn was beginning to crack the eastern sky as they made Franklin, four miles away, and Quantrill was worried that daylight would be upon them before they could strike their target. He arranged his command four abreast and urged the column on at a gallop.

As they drew upon the farm of Joseph Stone, the guerrillas paused while William Gregg pulled Stone from his bed and, so as to not cause any noise, beat him to death with a musket. Stone had caused some trouble for one or another of the raiders in Independence when war broke out.

Finally they mounted the rise just beyond Franklin and drew within sight of the city, the whitewashed buildings showing in the smoky Kaw Valley dawn, and the raiders paused for a moment. There was talk of turning back, now that the free state stronghold lay before them, but Quantrill would have none of it.

"Boys, this is the home of Jim Lane and that damned Jennison," he called from the saddle. "Remember that in hunting us they would have shot us down like dogs, white flag or no. Remember that they killed your women and intend to drive what families you have left from their homes. We are here for the men only; no one is to harm any woman or child. Unfurl the banner."

A black flag was broken out and passed up to the head of the column. The flag, which had been prepared during the guerrillas' war council, was to be the battlefield opposite of the white flag: no quarter sought or given, it declared.

"What time is it?" Quantrill asked George Todd.

Todd produced his pocket watch and replied that it was coming up on five o'clock.

"It's nearly past time," Quantrill said. "We should have already taken the city by now. Today is what? Friday? Well, that at least is good. Friday, you know—the day Adam was created, the day Jesus was crucified, the day that the dead will be called to the last judgment."

Quantrill drew his revolver and gave his final order: "Kill every man big enough to carry a gun."

He spurred his horse forward, and to a man the column followed after.

22

BILL ANDERSON, his dark hair flying from beneath his slouch hat, was alternately crying and mumbling Bible verses as the raiders swept into town from the southeast. Zachary Fenn had turned back his cloak to allow access to his revolvers, and blood ran down his arms from fresh cuts on his forearms. Patrick Fenn rode close by his brother, suddenly afraid at the fury with which the column descended on the town. The raiders had been taut and silent as they made the long ride across enemy territory, but now the tension broke in Rebel yells and demonic whoops as the riders galloped past sleeping houses toward the business district.

As planned, two detachments broke from the main column at the intersection of Rhode Island and Quincy streets. One squad raced to secure the ferry landing while the other made for the summit of Mt. Oread to the southwest, the tallest hill around, to stand watch for Union troops. Not far away two guerrillas broke away and bore down on the home of Reverend S.S. Snyder, which had been marked on the death maps. Snyder, who served as a lieutenant in the Second Colored Regiment, was shot dead as he sat milking a cow.

Zachary stayed with Quantrill as the main column turned north onto Massachusetts Street, the city's major thoroughfare, broad enough to accommodate six riders abreast. The riders galloped through the middle of a small tent camp where a score of recruits lay sleeping. Revolvers cracked as the young men pitched half-dressed from their tents, and seventeen of them lay dead by the time the raiders passed. The Reverend Larkin Skaggs paused long enough at the remains of the camp to tear down an American flag from a wooden staff, then raced after the rest, the flag tied to the tail of his horse and dragging in the dirt. Most of the black recruits at another camp, further down the street, heard the shooting and the screams and managed to escape into the brush.

After gunning down the recruits, the riders continued on down Massachusetts Street to the business district. Shop windows collapsed in a hail of gunfire and several early risers were shot dead as they appeared on the sidewalk in front of their stores to see what the commotion was about. The raiders swept all the way down Massachusetts to the river, making certain there was no hidden garrison of troops, and there Quantrill turned his horse and shouted the order to take the hotel.

The raiders converged at the Eldridge House, at the corner of Massachusetts and Winthrop. The four-story brick hotel was the headquarters for the state provost marshal's office and was the most defensible building in town. Quantrill was worried that the defenders might barricade themselves inside for a prolonged siege, and he had already gotten a bellyful of fortified brick structures.

Hundreds of guerrillas waited on their horses outside of the hotel while Quantrill studied the situation. There seemed to be no activity at the hotel, but Quantrill was anxious. At any minute he expected a barrage to begin from the upper floors. A window banged open and a dozen revolvers aimed and cocked before a white bedsheet appeared and the men were ordered to hold their fire.

"Is Quantrill with you?" an unseen man called from the window.

"News spreads fast," the guerrilla leader remarked and a dozen raiders around him laughed. Then he shouted: "Who are you?"

"Captain Banks, the provost marshal," the man answered. "Will you come forward, Mr. Quantrill?"

"It's *Colonel* Quantrill."

"Will you come forward, Colonel Quantrill?"

Quantrill nudged his horse through the crowd of raiders and drew up to the front of the hotel.

"I am here," he said. "Show yourself."

Banks raised his head above the windowsill.

"I see you," Quantrill said. "What do you want?"

"We are prepared to surrender the hotel if you will assure us that the guests will go unharmed."

Quantrill sat quietly on his horse for a moment, thinking it over. He leaned down and asked some of the men to reconnoiter the rear of the hotel for activity, to help determine if the offer was a hoax. While the squad rode to the rear of the building a gong sounded in the hotel's main lobby, and the revolvers were once again raised as Quantrill motioned for the raiders to draw back, ready for an attack.

"We are not going to fire!" Banks shouted. "That was a gong to wake those who are still asleep in the hotel. It is not an order to fire!"

Quantrill held out his hand and motioned for the men to lower their weapons.

"Will you agree to the terms we have offered?" Banks shouted. "We are prepared to immediately surrender the hotel. Will you promise not to harm the guests? We have not a single weapon among us. They are all locked up in the armory."

"I accept," Quantrill shouted back. The guerrillas cheered the surrender of the hotel. He dismounted and handed his reins to one of the men, and he indicated that Zachary and Patrick and five of the others were to accompany him into the hotel.

"The rest of you have your orders," Quantrill called to the others. "Go to it, and be quick about it. Remember, no quarter." The raiders dissolved into groups of six or eight men and, clutching their maps, set out for their targets.

The twenty-six-year-old guerrilla leader paused at the entrance to the hotel. He ran a hand over the growth of beard that had sprung up on the two-day ride from Missouri. He adjusted his black slouch hat with the gold braid, smoothed his dove-colored pants, and knocked some of the dust from his brown shirt. There were four Colt revolvers in his wide belt.

Quantrill strode past the shops that occupied the first floor of the hotel and went to the staircase leading to the sleeping rooms above.

"We intend to burn this hotel directly," he called up the stairs. "You have a few minutes to get yourselves together. My men will be passing among you shortly, and if you value your lives you will not resist."

Quantrill stayed at the bottom of the stairs while he ordered his

men to relieve the guests of their money and valuables. George
Todd came, pushing a man at gunpoint in front of him. Todd was
wearing a new Union officer's jacket with captain's bars on the
shoulders that he had taken from Banks, the provost marshal.
Todd's prisoner smiled when he saw Quantrill and he stuck out
his hand.

"Don't you know me?" he asked. "I'm Arthur Spicer, and I
knew you when we called you Charley Hart."

"It doesn't matter now what they called me," Quantrill said,
refusing to shake hands.

"We found him outside and I thought he was one of the prisoners trying to escape," Todd said, "so I didn't know whether you
wanted me to shoot him or not."

"He's not one of the guests," Quantrill replied. "He runs an
illegal saloon down the street, and when I lived in Lawrence before the war his brother Newell treated me roughly. No, I don't
want you to shoot him. Take him outside and get him a horse.
He's going to show us around the town."

Todd dragged Spicer back outside.

"It is fortunate for us," Quantrill remarked, "that the town fathers have sought to keep the evil of guns instead of hard liquor
away from their good citizens."

Zachary and Patrick took the second floor and passed among
the guests, gathering up their money and jewelry and placing it in
Patrick's hat. At the end of the north wing they were confronted
by a locked door, and Zachary pounded on it with the butt of his
revolver.

"Come out," Zachary said. "Colonel Quantrill has agreed to
spare your lives, but only if you surrender peaceably."

There was no response from behind the door.

"Have it your way," Zachary said, and fired three shots through
the door. A yelp was heard on the other side. The door opened
and three men filed out, one of them limping from a wound that
stained his white trousers red. Patrick relieved them of their cash,
rings, and watches.

"Quit your whimpering," Zachary told the wounded man. "It
ain't nothing but a scratch. Now get yourselves down the stairs to
the main hall with the others."

When all of the rooms had been searched, and the fifty-odd
hotel guests had been assembled in the lobby, Quantrill appeared

among them and announced that Lawrence was wholly in the hands of his men. Then Quantrill passed among his prisoners, shaking hands with a few old acquaintances that dared to congratulate the guerrilla on what was surely his finest victory.

"Yes," Quantrill said, "the city has been taken without a shot being fired in opposition."

He assured them that he had given his word as to their personal safety. Then Quantrill abruptly walked out of the lobby, leaving the prisoners to the handful of guards, and he ordered Zachary and Patrick to set fire to the storefronts on the hotel's ground floor.

Zachary kicked in the door of the law office and took the tops from the lamps and poured coal oil over the desks and papers, then set a match to them. Patrick smashed the drugstore's windows and took bottles of alcohol from the shelves and emptied their contents onto the wooden floor. Before he lit the alcohol he filled his pockets with tobacco and patent medicines and rolls of bandages and other items he thought the guerrillas might need.

When smoke began curling up into the second floor, the guards moved their prisoners out of the hotel and across the street into the weather-beaten earthworks that had been thrown up during the worst of the border war seven years before. During that fracas, in 1856, the first hotel operated by Colonel S.W. Eldridge—then called the Free State Hotel and on the same spot as the current affair—was burned to the ground by the pro-slavery faction.

Two of the prisoners carried Major F.B. Bancroft between them in an upholstered chair. He'd been badly wounded at Vicksburg and had returned home to Kansas to die. As they crossed the street toward the earthworks, Bancroft saw the Reverend Larkin Skaggs ride past. Skaggs was taking swigs from a bottle of stolen whiskey and was amusing himself by wheeling and dancing his horse while a badly stained and tattered American flag dragged behind. Bancroft, who was so weak that he had been unable to speak so far that morning, rose in the chair and pointed.

"God damn them," Bancroft said, "they are dragging my flag in the dust."

One of the raiders pointed a revolver in Bancroft's face and threatened to shoot him if he did not remain quiet, but it was an unnecessary gesture, because Bancroft could say no more.

Zachary and Patrick, their arsonist work finished, strode across

Massachusetts Street to reclaim their horses. Patrick spun on his heel in the middle of the street, taken aback by the scene around him.

In addition to the smoke now pouring from the Eldridge House, stores on both sides of Massachusetts were blazing. The windows of the two newspaper offices, the *Kansas Tribune* and the *Lawrence Republican,* had been shattered and the type scattered into the street. Men were carrying coats and other items from the clothing store on the corner, and provisions from the grocery store. They paid no attention to the dead men that dotted the sidewalk on both sides of the street, except occasionally to pitch the corpses into the burning buildings. Before setting fire to the saloons, the guerrillas had liberated the inventories and soon many of the roughest men were already staggering drunk.

"It is hell on earth," Patrick said.

"Yes," Zachary said, "isn't it?"

Quantrill had again mounted his horse, and when he saw that the guards had congregated the prisoners in the center of the old earthworks, he dashed over.

"I promised these folks that they would be protected," Quantrill said, "and I mean to keep my word. It is too open here for them, for the men are eager to shoot anything that wears pants."

Then he addressed the prisoners: "All of you go over to the City Hotel, and stay in it, and you will be safe. Nathan Stone, the landlord of the hotel, was kind to me years ago, and I have promised him protection. Once you are there, do not attempt to go into the street."

The guards began marching their prisoners toward the river, where the brown, two-story City Hotel stood near the ferry landing.

Quantrill went back to his squad in front of the burning Eldridge House and was satisfied to find Spicer mounted and waiting for him.

"What time is it?" Quantrill asked Todd.

"Five-thirty," Todd looked at his watch and replied.

"Are you prepared to follow orders or to face the consequences?" Quantrill demanded of Spicer.

"I am," Spicer said.

"I am glad that we understand one another," Quantrill said.

"Now, your first task is to take us to the new house built by Jim Lane."

James Lane had been awakened by the first volley of pistol shots. Suspecting that Quantrill had indeed come back to Lawrence, he took an axe and knocked the nameplate from his front door and then fled, in his nightshirt, to the cornfield behind the house.

Followed by Quantrill and his squad, Arthur Spicer rode to the home on Henry Street, seven blocks west of Massachusetts, and said flatly, "Here."

Quantrill dismounted and directed his men around to the rear of the house. He rapped at the front door and removed his hat when Mary Lane opened it.

"I am here to pay my respects to your husband," he said.

"He's not here."

"Do not lie to me."

"See for yourself," the woman offered, stepping aside.

"Search the house," Quantrill told the rest of his squad, and they rushed inside. Quantrill waited in the parlor, examining the piano that Lane had carted away from the sacking of Osceola and fingering the gold sword and the brigade flag that hung from the wall. When his men reported that Lane could not be found, Quantrill directed them to take the sword and the flag.

"Break up the furniture and smash the piano," Quantrill said, "and then burn the house."

Quantrill stood in the yard while the destruction and arson were undertaken. Mary Lane stood close by, watching as the torches were thrown among the pieces of furniture that would now serve as kindling.

"Tell the general that I am sorry I missed him," Quantrill told her. "Tell him that I have settled accounts with him for Osceola. Give him my compliments and say that I am very anxious to meet with him personally."

"I'm sure that Mr. Lane will be more than willing to accommodate you under different circumstances," she said, "but it is inconvenient this morning."

Quantrill mounted his horse.

"I am going to the City Hotel to have breakfast with my friend Nathan Stone," Quantrill told Todd. "Use Spicer as a guide to some of the other names on the list, and have the men continue their work. Report to me shortly."

Bill Anderson kicked in the front door of the house, with Patrick and Zachary close behind. Tears brimmed in Anderson's eyes and his face was flushed, as if he were drunk, but he had not taken a single drink that morning.

At the bottom of the stairs stood a man with his shirttails hanging over his pants. Next to him stood his wife, holding a child of two in her arms, and holding tight to her skirts was a little girl.

"Don't any of you move," Anderson raged, waving his pistol in one hand and clutching a bundle of matches in the other.

"Let the women and children go, Bill," Zachary said.

The women and the two children took a few steps toward the door, and Anderson raised his pistol. The man calmly watched the pistol come up and, although Anderson's intention was obvious, he did not cry out or beg for mercy, but looked at his family and smiled. Patrick jumped as the shot rang out and the man was knocked against the stairs. His shirt was puckered just above his stomach and a blossom of red appeared. Anderson emptied the revolver, took Zachary's gun from his hand, and began to fire it as well into the man, who was now slumped at the base of the stairs. Blood and bone splattered the wall behind him.

Gunsmoke filled the room. The children were shrieking and the woman put down the toddler and fell to the floor beside her husband.

Zachary reached out his hand and gripped the pistol Anderson held, his thumb jamming the action. He took the gun and stuck it back in his belt. He looked at Patrick, whose face was white.

"Edward," the woman cried over the body of her husband. "Please God, this cannot be happening. Edward, get up. Please. The children need you. *Edward.*"

Anderson was shaking as he struck a match against the door frame. The woman pleaded for Anderson to let her remove the body of her husband before the house was burned, but Anderson refused.

"Why have you done this?" she cried. "What in God's name have we done?"

"An eye for an eye," Anderson said as the match burned down between his fingers. "Your men have done this to our families, and worse. And because you are flying a damned Union flag from the top of your woodshed out back."

"A flag?" the woman asked. "The one out back? My God, the children were playing *soldier* with that flag a few days ago. That is why you have destroyed us? Because of children at play? What kind of demons are you?"

She threw herself at Anderson, but Patrick caught her by the waist and carried her outside. She dug her nails into Patrick's cheeks. The terrified little girl picked up the toddler and followed her mother outside.

Anderson was ranting, and crying again, and he began kicking over furniture and pulling pictures from the wall. He struck another match and tossed it into some drapes covering the front window. Shortly the house was engulfed.

The woman had taken her children across the street and now lay with them in a grassy ditch as they helplessly watched their home burn. Patrick sat on his horse and looked from them to the house and back. His cheeks were a lattice of crimson welts.

"How can you stand to do this work?" Patrick asked. "How could you watch that man be shot down in front of his family? What about the *children*? I understand we're after Lane and the others, but this man didn't even look like a soldier."

"It doesn't matter," Zachary said. "He was a Kansan."

"You are my brother and I will ride with you until we are clear of this. I will rob stores and burn buildings and fight soldiers, for that is what I joined for. But I refuse to shoot fathers down in front of their children."

"Then you are weaker than they," Zachary said.

Patrick reached out and grabbed his sleeve.

"This won't bring Sarah back," Patrick said. "Nothing will. And now nothing will bring that man back to his children. This isn't war, it's butchery."

Zachary's eyes softened for a moment, then he angrily shook his arm loose from Patrick's grasp and looked away.

"Zach," Patrick said sadly, "I don't know you anymore."

23

J ENNY WAS IN THE KITCHEN when she heard the front door open. Little Frank was playing with a bowl and a spoon on the kitchen floor, and she smiled at him as she dried her hands on a towel.

"Fitz?" she called. "We're in the kitchen."

When there was no answer she walked cautiously from the kitchen into the great room. The door was shut and no one was about. She walked to the base of the stairs and called up.

"Fitz? Are you here?"

There was no answer, and she began to grow more afraid. She turned to go back to the kitchen to be with Little Frank, and she gasped in surprise when she saw the man blocking the doorway. He was a large man, with coarse brown hands and an unruly beard. He wore greasy clothes and had a knife and a revolver in his belt.

"I'm sorry," Jenny said. "I did not hear you knock."

"That's because I didn't knock," Jake Herd said. "I don't usually, not when I intend on robbing a place. I didn't expect to find anything as pretty as you here."

Jenny stepped backward, but he grabbed her wrist.

"Where're you going?"

"Uncle Fitz is here with me," Jenny said. "He's right outside chopping wood, and he has his rifle with him. If I scream he will come in here and shoot you."

"I don't believe there's anybody here with you, excepting for that brat on the floor," Herd said. Then he squinted and looked at her curiously. Still holding her wrist in a crushing grip, he took a leather case from his pocket and looked at the daguerreotype inside.

"You're her," he said, holding the picture up. "I've been looking for you for a long, long time. Somebody killed my brother and my cousin on the old Sante Fe Trail near Lawrence, and they left this behind. What do you know about it?"

"That's not me," Jenny lied. "I've never seen that before in my life. I don't know what you're talking about."

"Yes, you do," Herd said. "I can see it in your eyes. You know exactly what I'm talking about, and you know who killed Jess and Jeremy. And you're going to tell me before I'm through—yes, you'll be begging to tell me."

Jenny turned her face but Herd grasped the back of her head and jerked her hair back. He kissed her and his breath stank of liquor and rotten teeth. She fought against him, but he pinned her against the wall and ripped the buttons of her dress away with a sweep of his hand.

"You'll be sorry for this," she managed, but Herd just laughed. He took the knife from his belt and ran the point down between her breasts, then cut away her corset. Jenny began to cry as he thrust his dirty hands inside. His nails cut into her tender flesh and she grimaced.

"What are you squirming for?" he asked. "This is nothing. You had better enjoy this. Because after I have had my fill of you, I am going to tie you down and start cutting that pretty skin away, a piece at a time, just like you would skin a cat. By the time I cut your eyelids away you'll be reciting every verse you learned in grammar school and pleading with me to kill you."

Jenny screamed and Herd just laughed at her.

He pulled her down to the floor by her hair, then unbuckled his belt and let it fall aside. He pulled the rest of her clothes away and was attempting to hold her down and unbutton his trousers at the same time when Jenny's eyes widened and looked over his shoulder.

"What?" he asked, and turned his head.

Fitz had crept in as quiet as an Indian and was standing over them with the chopping axe raised above his head. Herd groped for his gun but the axe was already tracing an arc down, and the blade sank into his forehead with a thud. Blood splattered over Jenny's face.

Fitz kicked the body away from Jenny. After making sure that Herd was quite dead, he retrieved a quilt from the downstairs bedroom and threw it over Jenny, then picked her up in his arms like a child. He took her to the bed and wiped the blood from her face and held her while she cried.

"Are you hurt or just scared?" Fitz asked.

"Scared," Jenny said, trembling.

Fitz nodded. "Was he alone?"

Jenny looked at him.

"This is important. Was he alone?"

"I think so," she said at length. "At least I didn't see anybody else . . . Why isn't Frank here? Why doesn't he come back? Doesn't he care about me?"

"He cares," Fitz said.

"Little Frank," Jenny said suddenly. "Where—"

"He's fine. He's still playing in the kitchen. I'm going to go look after him now."

"Bring him to me," Jenny said.

Later Fitz dragged the body out of the kitchen door to the barn, where he dug a shallow grave in a corner, away from prying eyes. He threw the body in and scooped the dirt in around it, then piled stones and boards over the spot so that dogs wouldn't be digging there.

He kept Herd's revolver.

24

THE CITY HOTEL was in full view of the squad of federal soldiers that stood near the ferry on the north bank of the Kaw and watched telltale columns of dark smoke rising in the hot morning air. The soldiers had taken scattered potshots at the guerrillas on the opposite bank, but their effectiveness across the quarter-mile expanse of water was negligible. Soon they simply leaned on their rifles and waited uneasily for troops they hoped were coming from Kansas City.

Inside the hotel, Quantrill had finished his plate of bacon and eggs and now he held a cup of black coffee in his hands, his elbows propped on the fresh linen tablecloth. From the open window came the smell of smoke and the sound of revolvers popping, but he did not let it distract him from his conversation with Nathan Stone or his pretty dark-eyed daughter, Lydia. Was it only yesterday or a lifetime ago, Quantrill wondered, when he had taken sick to his room in the hotel and Lydia had patiently nursed him back to health. Like many others, she had been taken with the young man's good looks and easy charm. Quantrill had presented her with a diamond ring as a token of his gratitude, and she promised to keep it for life.

While Quantrill was vainly searching for Jim Lane that morning, drunken Larkin Skaggs had strode into the City Hotel on unsteady legs and robbed some of the guests. The Reverend Skaggs had taken the ring at gunpoint from Lydia, despite her warning that Quantrill himself had given it to her, and when the guerrilla chief arrived at the hotel for breakfast she lost no time in recounting what had happened and identifying Skaggs. Quantrill immediately sent for the reverend and forced him to return the ring with an apology. The ring again sparkled on Lydia's hand as she and Quantrill chatted, but as Skaggs reeled out into the street he swore that "the bitch would be sorry."

Lydia's hand trembled slightly as she poured Quantrill more coffee. She did not know if she sat with him because of the friendship they once had, to secure the safety of the guests and keep her father's hotel from the flames, or because she was terribly curious about what this once quiet young man had become. In any case, it was far better than cowering in her room.

Quantrill ran a hand over his stubble and apologized to Lydia for his rough appearance.

"Life in the brush is difficult and I am not often prepared for the gentle company of women," he said. "How I miss the days of my youth when my heaviest concern was how to express my gratitude to angels such as you."

"What has happened to you, Charley?" Lydia asked. She knew the name he now went by—his real name, many said—but she could not think of him as such and he did not correct her. "You were such a sensitive soul when you were under our roof, and now you have come back at the head of a band of demons. I can scarcely believe what my eyes tell me is taking place beyond those windows."

"I was a sensitive fool," Quantrill said and smiled sadly. "Do you know I once wrote my sister and pressed wildflowers in the pages of the letter to show her the beauty of Kansas?"

"Yes, you told me once."

"Wildflowers," Quantrill said. "Imagine that. What should I include if I were to write my sister or my mother of Kansas this morning? How can you press lies between the pages of a letter, how can you distill deceit? Betrayal tastes like burnt embers in my mouth."

"But who has been betrayed?" Lydia asked.

"I do not write letters to my mother any longer," Quantrill continued. "It is too difficult. What can one say of this business? The tide has turned and the cause in the East is lost. Vicksburg, Gettysburg. But war is destruction, and this war is not played out. There are debts to pay and the last chapter has not been written. And yet—"

"Yes?"

"I think I would give it all up for the comfort of a soft cheek and the promise of a warm embrace. To have a home, to truly have a *home,* and a family I could call my own."

"Charley, won't you tell me what has become of you?" Lydia asked, touching his hand. "Please answer me, if only out of respect for what we once meant to each other."

Quantrill looked at her from beneath sleepy blue lids. He turned his face toward the window and breathed deeply of the tainted morning air.

"Destiny," he said at last. "Destiny has found me."

The livery stable behind the Eldridge House had not yet burned and Zachary reined to a halt in front of it and peered within. The door had been left open after the horses and carriages had been stolen, and something hanging upon the wall had caught his eye as he rode past. He dismounted and walked Raven into the stable.

Patrick, who was not speaking to his brother, waited astride his horse.

On the wall hung a set of harness bells, set aside for use with a team that pulled a sleigh when snow was upon the ground. Zachary took the bells down from their peg and examined them. They were silver and finely worked. It took but a moment to attach the bells to Raven's bridle, and they rang satisfyingly with each dip of the horse's head.

Zachary struck a match against the rough wood of the stable wall and tossed the flame into a bed of straw. He swung into Raven's saddle and rode outside to the rhythm of the bells.

Cole Younger was sitting on his horse and reloading his pistols when Zachary came out of the livery stable. He looked curiously at the harness bells and laughed.

"What in hell are those bells for?" he asked.

Zachary didn't answer.

Patrick shook his head.

"I'm sorry, Cole," Patrick said. "I'm afraid that Zach's mind has slipped with the shock of losing Sarah. Our Uncle Fitz used to tell this story—"

"What's he doing now?"

Zach was taking the books from his saddlebags and, one by one, was throwing them into the flames of the livery stable. When he had come to the last book he placed his hand on the cover lovingly and then let it fall open to a well-thumbed page. Zachary tore the page out, folded it and tucked it into his pocket, then threw that book into the flames as well.

Zachary looked up at Cole and his brother.

"I get no joy from reading," he said, and rode on.

Colonel John D. Holt rode down Rhode Island Street on a horse he had stolen from the livery stable near the Eldridge House. Under his arm was tucked a box of cigars. A man standing in the front yard of his home recognized Holt's yellow-trimmed jacket to be that of a regular Confederate officer and he hailed him. The man was emboldened because Holt's belted revolver was clean of any telltale powder residue.

"Pardon me," the man called. "You are a colonel, no? Could you spare a moment for me?"

Holt brought the horse to a stop.

"What do you want?" he asked. "You are liable to get yourself shot standing in the open."

"My name is Henry Clarke, and I own—I *owned*—the furniture store down on Massachusetts. The guerrillas have already robbed my wife and I, and they have promised to return to burn our home. It is the only thing we have left, and I throw myself upon your mercy."

Holt sighed and looked at the agitated man.

"I was a merchant as well," Holt said. "I owned a first-rate hardware store there and was quite happy before Doc Jennison and his Jayhawkers burned it to the ground. After that I joined Sterling Price and accepted a commission, and for some months now have been in the brush throughout northern Missouri recruiting a company. Quantrill invited me to accompany him here to christen the recruits, and I am sorry to say that I accepted the invitation. I fear that we are only sowing more of the dragon's teeth."

Holt opened the box and offered Clarke a cigar. Then Holt took one for himself as well and they smoked and talked of business, as if nothing out of the ordinary were happening around them.

"We nearly went bankrupt before the war came," Clarke said, smoke curling from the corner of his mouth. "It looked as if Lawrence would not economically survive the ravages of '59 and '60.

These people that came here were merchants and politicians and clerks, not farmers. The drought nearly wiped them out and no one had money. Then, after the war broke, there were so many troops passing through and so much activity that it was a godsend to our little store. But what the war has given, I suppose, the war has taken away."

Holt nodded.

"You look like you are hungry, Colonel," Clarke said. "Would you like to come inside and have some breakfast? Food is one of the few things that we still possess."

"I'm afraid not," Holt said. "It would not be appropriate for me to leave my post. There is much to be done—we must be prepared to leave in a short while, and the troops are still scattered. But I am starving. There has been precious little time to eat in the last few days."

"Then let me fix you a plate and bring it out to you. Eggs and ham, perhaps some boiled potatoes. You can sit on your horse and eat."

Holt deliberated for a moment.

"If you would be so kind," he said, "I will attempt to offer your home my protection."

The man walked back to the house, and in a few minutes he came back carrying the food and a cup of coffee. A group of Quantrill's men were tearing up the street, and one of them spotted Clarke and bore down upon him, revolver poised.

Holt drew his own weapon and fired into the air.

"Leave that man be," Holt ordered. "He is bringing me my breakfast."

"Sorry, Colonel," the guerrilla said. His hands were blackened with gunpowder, and there was a black streak across his nose where he had scratched it. "I did not realize he was in your charge. Say, would there be more where that came from? We are powerfully hungry and have not been able to find a bite to eat all morning."

"Yes, there is more," Clarke said.

Soon there were thirty guerrillas sitting in the yard, and although the eggs and ham were quickly consumed Clarke fed the rest with boiled potatoes.

When Holt had finished his plate he handed it back to Clarke.

"Thank you," Holt said. He took a slip of paper from his jacket and wrote his name and address with a pencil and handed it to the man. "I would be pleased to correspond with you when this war is over, should the end find us both among the living. Your kindness will long be remembered."

As Holt rode away, he left orders with the men still in the yard that Clarke was not to be molested and that his home was to remain intact.

A stolen carriage pulled by an equally stolen team of white horses pulled up to the City Hotel and Quantrill said goodbye to Lydia and her father. He stepped outside, tipped his black slouch hat to the ladies that were gathered at the windows, and bid them farewell. Then he stepped up into the carriage and told the driver to take him to the top of Mt. Oread. The carriage pulled away with a squad of guerrillas following.

The carriage clattered up Massachusetts Street. Many of the buildings had already collapsed into heaps of flaming timbers, strewing debris into the street. Bodies lay singly, or in groups of twos and threes, and rarely had the corpses been allowed to keep their boots. The sickeningly sweet smell of burned flesh was common and here and there blackened corpses could be seen lying rigidly among the embers.

The carriage turned off Massachusetts to the west and pulled up the slope of the hill. The day was growing quite hot and Quantrill fanned himself with his hat. At the crest of the hill the carriage stopped and Quantrill alighted and stood on top of the broken-down remains of the free-state fortifications that had been hastily thrown up during the territorial years.

Below him lay Lawrence, and from every corner of the city flames threw billows of smoke into the air. The ruin of the business district looked like an ugly scar pointing toward the river, and ash drifted lazily over the Kaw valley. Groups of riders were on every street, still searching for those who had escaped the first assault and rounding up horses and wagons with which to carry away their loot. The death lists had been cast aside and now the riders, especially those that were drunk, were shooting down men and boys who had been driven from their hiding places by the flames. Scores of others already lay dead in the rubble, burned to death where they lay terrified beneath their homes, or suffocated in wells. Even from this distance the anguished cries of the women could be heard.

"Colonel Quantrill," one of the men with a spyglass said. "There's a column of dust to the east. It could be a company of Yankee cavalry."

Quantrill took the spyglass and looked for himself. There was indeed a plume of dust on the eastern horizon, as if thrown up by horses, but it was impossible to tell who or what was causing it.

"What time is it?" Quantrill asked.

A half-dozen guerrillas produced stolen pocket watches. Eight-thirty, they said.

"I believe we are near to wearing out our welcome," Quantrill said. "Back to town, and gather the men together. We will leave before the clock strikes nine."

Each time the Reverend Larkin Skaggs struck a match the woman inside the house would blow it out, and in his drunken confusion he was becoming exasperated.

"You are the queerest woman I have ever met," he said and, with his bundle of matches exhausted, gave up trying to burn the home. He stumbled back out into the yard and unsteadily mounted his horse. He was uncertain of which part of town he was in, then he spied the two-story City Hotel on the corner and he remembered his oath.

He rode up to the front of the hotel and dismounted, nearly sank to his knees in the dirt, then pitched forward to the entrance. Quantrill had urged the prisoners to remain within the hotel, but the guards he had left soon took off also as their commander made his journey to the top of Mt. Oread. Not long after other guerrillas came and ordered the prisoners outside, and when they began shooting them down the remainder fled out the back windows and somehow convinced the ferry operator on the north side of the Kaw to come over and rescue them. But Nathan Stone and his daughter had remained, and when Skaggs saw the old man standing in the lobby of the hotel, he pulled his revolver and shot him dead. Lydia threw herself on the body of her father and the Reverend Larkin Skaggs staggered back into the street.

He mounted his horse, but was unsure of which way to go. The main body of guerrillas seemed to have already left the town.

From behind he heard shouts and curses from a group of Delaware Indians and federal soldiers who had dared to cross the river. Skaggs finally got his bearings and raced south on Massachusetts Street, pursued by the mob, and had almost reached the city limits when a shot was fired by a boy with an old gun. The ball struck Skaggs in the shoulder and he was knocked from his horse into the dust. In an instant the mob was upon him, and an Indian named White Turkey shot an arrow into the drunken preacher, piercing his heart. As Skaggs drew his last breath the Indian leaned over him and cut away his scalp.

The boy who had shot him stood over the body and spat. His name was Billy Speer, and the guerrillas had killed his brothers John and Robert.

All the clothes were stripped from Skaggs' body and he was tied behind a nag and dragged through the streets, just as he had done to Bancroft's flag. Then they threw him into the deep ravine that bisected the town and there his body was left to rot for the winter.

When Quantrill and his band rode out of Lawrence at nine o'clock that morning, they left behind one hundred and fifty dead men and boys; there were eighty widows and two hundred fatherless children; and one hundred and eighty-five buildings, including most of the business district, lay in ashes.

Quantrill's losses amounted to a handful of wounded men, scores with throbbing hangovers, and only one dead guerrilla: the Reverend Larkin Skaggs, whom Quantrill would have killed anyway upon hearing of the death of his friend Nathan Stone.

The dust that Quantrill had seen from the top of Mt. Oread was raised by two hundred and fifty mounted troops under the command of a Major Plumb, who from Olathe had seen dark smoke on the horizon and surmised that Quantrill had struck Lawrence. James Lane, by now dressed in an ill-fitting suit of farm clothes and riding a plug horse after escaping overland from the cornfield, joined the pursuing column south of Lawrence. Although the federals had closed to within a quarter of a mile of the guerrillas at one point, the troopers repeatedly refused to obey commands to attack. The remainder of the chase deteriorated into no more than harassment for Quantrill as he at first drove south, then turned east for the protection of Missouri.

By the next day six thousand soldiers were searching for Quantrill, including General Ewing himself with five Ohio companies outfitted at Fort Leavenworth, but the guerrilla leader and his command were already safely in the woods of Cass County. Lane met Ewing six miles inside Missouri—where the trail seemingly evaporated—and complained bitterly of Ewing's failure to protect Lawrence.

"When are you going to enforce the order to move everyone out of the border counties?" Lane, who was still dressed in the baggy farm clothes, ranted. "Do you need any further cause? How many more massacres will it take? Move them out, kill the guerrillas' base of support, and then burn every home to the ground. You will be finished in politics and in the military if you do not act *now*."

Like Quantrill, Ewing had come to Kansas from Ohio. He had practiced law in Leavenworth, rose in the Republican party with the help of his friend Jim Lane, and was named to the new state's supreme court. Through Lane's influence as a U.S. senator, Ewing had secured his present position as commander of the District of the Border. But Ewing had grown increasingly uncomfortable with Lane, and their friendship was beginning to chafe; he knew Lane to be a thief and an opportunist, but more recently, he began to suspect that Lane was slipping into madness. But voices were already clamoring for severe retaliation for the Lawrence raid, and many believed that Ewing was guilty of gross negligence in failing to protect the state from the invaders. Ewing believed the guerrillas had left him with no choice but to adopt Lane's scorched earth policy toward the border counties.

Lane largely authored General Order Number Eleven, which was issued from Ewing's headquarters on August 25, 1863—four days after the raid on Lawrence. The order called for the removal of every citizen living more than one mile from any military post in Cass, Bates, and Jackson counties, and half of Vernon County; it required the destruction of all homes, farms, and businesses in those areas, and any kind of grain or stores that might be of use to the guerrillas; and it gave the population fifteen days in which to comply, or to be considered outlaws and to be dealt with accordingly.

To help enforce the order—there were still doubts that Ewing was capable of carrying it out without help from Kansas—Charles R. "Doc" Jennison was authorized by Kansas Governor Thomas Carney to raise a regiment to "avenge the lawless sacking of Lawrence and to punish the Rebel invaders of our State."

25

September 1863

FITZ WATCHED the soldiers as they rode, two abreast, up the lane to the house. He was sitting in a wooden chair, his unlit pipe in his mouth, a folded Kansas City newspaper in his lap. It was a dark afternoon and a cool wind blew over the Little Shannon Valley from the northeast.

Fitz felt old. His hair had gotten considerably grayer since the war began, and hunger had withered his normally thin frame. He could tell from the aching of the arrowhead in his spine that the barometer was falling, and he hoped for rain.

The soldiers spread out, their Sharps rifles pointing up to the sky, and they hung back a few lengths as Jennison rode up. He sat in the saddle and regarded Fitz a few moments before he spoke.

"It is time, old man," Jennison said.

"I reckoned it was," Fitz said. "I've been watching the smoke from the fires as you came from Harrisonville. How many homes have you burned today? A dozen?"

"It is work that has long been overdue," Jennison said. "How many times have you hidden Quantrill and his murderers in your barn or nursed his wounded in your cellar? How many boys from this farm are with him now, plotting the murder of loyal Kansas men?"

"Not near enough, I allow."

"You are brazen enough for one who is facing the torch," Jennison said.

"I don't reckon I'll do any begging today," Fitz said.

"You had better clear away from that house."

"There's a woman and a child inside."

"Then you had better get the secesh bitch and her brat outside," Jennison said, "or we will burn them out. You have two minutes."

"You are sadly misinformed," Fitz said. "I hated that woman when my nephew brought her here because she was the staunchest fire-breathing abolitionist I had ever met. But I have grown to love her. She has stood with us and never once complained. She is the strongest person, man or woman, that I have ever known and she makes both of us seem like frightened children in comparison. God help us both when we are called to answer for our sins."

"I am not interested in your family history," Jennison said.

"Your kind never is," Fitz said.

"Your time is running out."

"Jenny," Fitz called softly.

Jenny opened the door a crack. She had watched the approach of the soldiers from the upstairs window and, when they had reached the house, she had listened behind the front door as they spoke to Fitz.

"Get Little Frank and come on outside," Fitz said.

"No," Jenny said.

"Honey, I don't want you to get hurt. Fetch Little Frank and your sack of things and wait for me in the yard, away from the house. Do it for me, child, because there is no reasoning with these reptiles."

Jenny closed the door. Fitz looked over the soldiers in the yard. There were at least thirty of them. They sat uncomfortably upon their tired mounts, their hands and faces blackened with smoke. Some of them were no older than Zachary, and Fitz suddenly felt sorry for them. It was the old men, Jennison and Lane and Ewing and the rest, that had stolen their youth and betrayed their innocence.

"Say, you wouldn't happen to have any tobacco, would you? I haven't had anything to smoke in ages. I would like to sit in this chair beside the house and have one last smoke before I give it up."

Jennison cursed, but a blond-headed boy dismounted and

walked over to Fitz. He offered a leather pouch of burley tobacco, and Fitz filled his pipe.

"A match?" Fitz asked.

"We have plenty of those," the boy said. Fitz struck the match on the leg of the chair and sucked flame into the pipe. "Where are you from, boy?"

"Lawrence."

Fitz nodded.

"Get back to your horse, Speer, before I bring you up on charges," Jennison snapped.

Jenny came outside, carrying Little Frank on her hip and gripping a grain sack containing a little food and some clothes. Fitz had told her to take only what she could carry, but it broke her heart to leave her trunks and books behind. Her face was close to breaking.

"It will be all right, dear," Fitz said.

"I'm not going to cry," Jenny said, biting her bottom lip. "I will not give them the satisfaction. I don't know where we are going to go, and I do not know how we will live. They have taken everything from us. But Frank will come for us in time, and until then I will not cry."

"Go on and wait by the fence," Fitz said. "I'll be along shortly."

"Let's go, old man," Jennison said. "You've had your talk and you've had your smoke, and you've wasted enough of our time. There are other Rebel nests waiting for us."

Fitz didn't move.

"You can fry, then," Jennison said, and ordered his men: "Burn the house."

The soldiers lit three oil-soaked torches. Jennison's head was turned, watching the men, when he heard the triple click of a .44-caliber revolver as Fitz brought it out of the folds of the newspaper.

Jennison snapped his head around and saw the bore of the revolver throw down upon him and Fitz pull the trigger. Paralyzed, he watched as the hammer fell. But instead of a roar there was only a weak pop as the percussion cap burst and Herd's gun misfired.

"Kill him!" Jennison screamed.

Fitz had the gun cocked again, but five Sharps rifles barked from among the soldiers. Three of the shots missed, but one struck Fitz in the thigh and another hit him in the chest. The revolver was jerked off target as this chamber ignited, and Jennison felt the ball graze his scalp.

Fitz had lunged for the doorway, but another volley smashed the door and frame to pieces and struck his back, propelling him into the great room. The revolver fell from his hand and he lay dying with his hand touching the hearthstone.

Jennison mopped at the blood running down his forehead with a handkerchief.

"What are you waiting on?" Jennison raged. "Throw those torches."

The soldiers tossed the torches through the open doorway.

Jenny sank down beside the fence. She had watched the scene play out before her without being able to speak or cry out, and now she watched as tongues of flame licked up the inside walls and dark smoke boiled from the top of the doorway. She held Little Frank, who had started crying and trembling when the shooting began, and she shielded his eyes as flames consumed Fitz's body.

"Go take care of the barn," Jennison said, and soon it was ablaze as well. "Don't leave anything standing."

In minutes they were gone, thundering back down the lane.

When they had long since passed out of sight it began to rain, large drops that splattered the ground and hissed when they struck the flames of the house. But the fire was raging and the rain did nothing to dampen the blaze.

The rain soaked Jenny's clothes and she wrapped Little Frank in her shawl. She looked around her, not knowing if she should stay and hope someone would come or if she should strike out on her own. But she did not know which way to go and she was so stricken with grief that her arms and legs felt too heavy to move, so she stayed by the fence and continued to watch the house burn.

She was alone, with a child to care for and little more than the clothes she wore, and she did not know if Frank or the other boys were alive or dead.

Tears mixed with the rain upon her cheeks.

Frank had attempted to resign his commission when news of the barracks collapse reached St. Louis, but his resignation was refused. A week later he deserted. He slipped aboard a steamboat that took him down the Missouri River to Jefferson City, but the pilot refused to go farther west. The guerrillas had taken to attacking boats when they stopped for fuel or ran aground on sand bars. In Jefferson City he boarded a train bound for Sedalia, but they hadn't made thirty miles before the engine huffed to a stop in front of a twisted pile of rails. The Rebels had torn up a section of the track and melted the rails over a huge fire. Frank bought a horse with the last of his money and set out overland, but his horse was shot from beneath him by a forward party and he escaped with his life only by diving into the river and hiding in a logjam. Later he was chased by a Union patrol, despite his uniform, because he didn't know the elaborate system of sign and countersign that had been employed on the border to guard against Rebels clad in blue. Finally he had taken to hiding in barns, stealing food, and moving only at night.

It had taken him three weeks to reach Cass County and by the time he did it was already called the Burnt District. He walked along roads that were no longer familiar to him and wandered across barren fields. The farms were all gone, the houses were burned, and the only thing left of the homesteads were the lonely chimneys—the Jennison Monuments. With fear growing inside of him he ran the last mile through the devastated Little Shannon Valley until he could at least see the hillside he had called home, but there was no house there any longer.

He stood amid the ruins of the house, walked among the charred rubble and asked himself a thousand times where Jenny and the others must have gone. Surely they were safe, he told himself. Surely Fitz had found them some clever hiding place, away from the guns and torches of the Jayhawkers.

Frank sat down on the hearth and placed his palm against the cool stones. He remembered how he had played there as a child, basking in the light and warmth of the firelight with his brothers. He longed for those simple days and he cursed himself for ever believing that he could leave and that the war would not come home. How could he ever have left his wife and child to the mercy of strangers?

His shoe brushed something hard and dirty white in the ashes, and his stomach turned to ice water. It was a skull. He gingerly picked it up and held it in both hands in front of him. The jawbone was missing and the crown was shattered. He did not know what a man or a woman's skull would look like, or how to judge the age when most of the teeth were missing, but he feared it was rather smallish.

Was it Jenny?

Were there other skulls among the ashes? A tiny one, perhaps?

He held the skull against his chest and prayed for forgiveness. Surely it had to be one of them. They would not have let the house be burned without a fight. Frank felt like such a fool. It should have been *his* skull lying in the ashes. He should have been the one who died trying to save the house.

"God," Frank said, looking heavenward. "Why have you allowed this to happen? What have we done to deserve this?"

Then he began to sob, and the answer came with terrible certainty to lodge within his heart. The tears that stung his eyes felt like the tears of a coward.

26

ZACHARY WAS STANDING PICKET on the outskirts of Quantrill's camp in Jackson County. He was hidden in the darkness at the head of a wooded hollow that led to the cave where Quantrill kept kegs of gunpowder that he and Andy Walker had stolen from an ammunition boat at the start of the war. The woods were dotted with guerrilla pickets, for a mile up and down the hollow, and nothing could move in or out of the area without Quantrill knowing about it. The Union authorities either did not know about the cave or, perhaps, were unprepared to cross the rugged terrain and lay siege to the fortress-like cavern in the rocky bluffs.

It was long past midnight and the night had been quiet. The stars shone brightly in the sky above but the moon was down, making the woods darker yet. Quantrill and his captains were still in the middle of a council to discuss plans to move the company south for the winter. Despite the devastation wrought by Order Number Eleven, Quantrill had continued to operate, harassing Kansas troops and attacking steamboats on the Missouri River. But the coming winter promised to be impossible to endure within the barren border counties.

Zachary leaned against a tree and folded his arms over his chest. It was boring work and he would much prefer riding flat-out against the enemy to this cat-and-mouse game in the dark. His mind drifted, and he began to think of Sarah again, and the pain swelled within him. He thought of the night under the full moon they had spent together on Sugar Creek—their only night —and only the bittersweet ache of longing remained. He longed for death to release him from the torment, but he was afraid to believe that he would be with her on the other side. So much had been taken from him that he no longer dared hope for comfort, even in death. Prayer was out of the question. Even if there was a God somewhere among those stars, he refused to bend his knee to the One that had allowed Sarah to be taken from him. The best that he could hope for was simply the absence of pain, to join the earth in forgetfulness and to sleep the dreamless sleep of the dead.

A twig snapping in the darkness brought his attention back and he stood like a statue against the tree. Another twig snapped, and then there was the sound of feet slipping over the leaves. Whoever it was was moving toward him. Zachary reckoned it could be a Union scout sent to reconnoiter the area in preparation for a before-dawn attack. His hand went to the butt of his revolver, but then he paused. It would be better to keep things quiet, and to find out exactly what the guerrillas were up against, before alerting the enemy with gunfire.

The sound of walking drew steadily closer, and presently Zachary could make out the dark shape of a man moving through the trees. Zachary let the man pass within three feet of where he stood before slipping up behind him. He clamped a hand over the intruder's mouth and pressed the point of the knife into the small of his back.

"If you make a sound I will cut out your kidneys and feed them to you," Zachary said. He was close enough now that he could see the man's uniform and the officer's bars on the shoulders. "Now, I'm going to let my hand away from your mouth, and I want you to tell me in a whisper who you are and what kind of strength is out there."

Zachary pulled his hand away.

The man spun and deflected the knife point with a downward blow of his left forearm, and at the same drove his right fist into Zachary's face. Zachary sprawled on his back in the leaves and grabbed the revolver from his belt, but the man kicked it away and drove his heel into Zachary's chest. The wind went out of him in a rush.

Zachary grabbed the man's foot with both hands and twisted. The man fell on his side to keep his ankle from being snapped. Zachary struggled to his knees and sucked air into his aching lungs. The man was halfway up when Zachary put his head down and charged into him, striking him in the stomach, and they went down again. Zachary clawed his way up and sat on the man's chest while he pummeled his face, but the man reached up with his legs and locked his feet around his neck, pulling him off backward.

Zachary's head struck the ground hard and lights flashed before his eyes, but he saw the man lunge for him and he kicked out. The heel of his boot sank into the man's groin and he fell heavily to the ground, his hands between his legs. He began to vomit.

Zachary found the revolver in the leaves and thumbed the hammer back as he pointed it at the man's head. Zachary was breathing heavily and he wiped the blood from the corner of his mouth with the back of his hand.

"You have one last chance before I blow your brains out," Zachary said. "Who the hell are you?"

The man coughed out a last mouthful and turned his eyes to Zachary. There was just enough starlight to make the suggestion of a face.

"Frank?" Zachary asked, and lowered the revolver.

He nodded, but still could not talk.

"I have taken an oath to kill anyone who supports the Union," Zachary said angrily. "I suppose you have come back home to lead Ewing to Quantrill's headquarters. Damn you, why couldn't you stay away? Now you have made me kill you."

Zachary knelt down and pressed the gun to Frank's temple. His right hand was shaking, and he placed his other hand around the grip to steady it.

Frank closed his eyes and waited for the report. He was still in agony. It felt as if his testicles had been kicked up into his throat.

Sweat rolled down Zachary's brow and into his eyes. He shook his head and blinked hard. *It won't bring Sarah back,* he heard Patrick say somewhere in a corner of his mind. *Nothing will.*

"Oh, hell," Zachary said, and drew away the gun. "I don't want to make a racket."

"I'm alone," Frank managed.

"So am I," Zachary said, and he suddenly handed the gun to Frank. "Kill me. I'm not even true to my oath and I'm no good to my fellows. If you won't shoot me, then take me back to Ewing and let him hang me. I can't stand this pain anymore. I want to die."

"I'm not going to shoot you," Frank said, sitting up. "And I'm not going to take you back to Ewing. Christ, Zach, I've deserted. They've burned the farm, Zach, and I think Jenny's dead. There's nothing left for me but to ride with you and Patrick."

"I'm sorry," Zachary said, and placed a hand on his brother's shoulder. The pain in Frank's voice had reached him as nothing else had since the day the barracks had collapsed. Zachary moaned and began to cry.

Frank laid the revolver aside and held his brother in his arms for the first time since the night their mother had died, when Zachary was eleven. Frank patted his back and stroked his hair and brushed the tears away with his palm.

"You mustn't ride with me," Zachary said. "They will catch us and hang all of us and then there will be no more Fenns left. You and Patrick have to get away."

"There's nowhere left to run," Frank said. "I aim to make a fight of it."

"There's Texas," Zachary said, and for the first time hope began to grow within him. "We are preparing to make for Texas for the winter. There's no Jayhawkers or Jim Lanes or Tom Ewings there. You and Patrick can be careful as we make our way down the border and through the Indian Nations until we reach Texas, and then you will be safe."

"Then we will make it together," Frank said.

Zachary nodded, but something told him he would never see Texas.

"You must get rid of that uniform before one of the boys shoots you," Zachary said. "It's a good thing that I was foolish enough to try to take you quiet, rather than snipe you as you walked past."

"It didn't feel too foolish to me," Frank said, grimacing. "I don't remember you ever hitting that hard—or that low."

"I never remembered you being that quick," Zachary said and grinned. "Besides, I think my jaw is dislocated, and that makes us even."

"Not quite," Frank said, shifting uncomfortably.

"Frank, you have to promise me something," Zachary said. "If I get killed—"

"You're not going to die."

"Cole Younger tells me that they buried Sarah in that little place on Sugar Creek where we had planned to homestead,"

Zachary said. "If I go under, I want to be buried there with her, even if you have to plant me where I fall and come back in a year or two and dig me up."

"I promise," Frank said, "but it's going to be a long, long time before I have to keep that promise. We Fenn brothers are going to beat this war. You wait and see."

There was a rude democracy in the bush and the guerrillas chose their own squad leaders—even Quantrill's command was subject to popular consent. Following his fury during the Lawrence raid, Zachary had found himself with his own group of raiders. The same was true of Bill Anderson, who had been an earnest but undistinguished rider before that August.

The boys accepted Frank simply as another Fenn brother, and if anyone knew of Frank's past service, they kept it to themselves. Frank was amazed to see how young the guerrillas were. Most were between fifteen and nineteen, and like Zachary wore their hair to their shoulders and delighted in the decorated shirts their mothers and sweethearts made for them. They were *children,* Frank thought, and gave a true meaning to the word guerrilla— the little warrior, a term that had been borrowed from the Spanish by Wellington in the Napoleonic wars. Frank, who was twenty-six, felt old in comparison, and he felt rather awkward taking orders from his youngest brother, who was not yet twenty.

"You just hang back and don't risk yourself any more than necessary," Zachary told him. "Fight like hell if you're in a corner, but don't go out of your way to show us how brave you are. That goes for you too, Patrick."

"I'll watch your back if you watch mine," Patrick said.

Although he was speaking again to him, Patrick still feared that Zachary might slip into the homicidal madness he had seen in Lawrence. But the reunion with Frank had seemed to restore some balance, despite the horrible news that accompanied him. It was painful for Patrick to imagine that the house where they grew up was no more, and that Jenny and the rest were probably dead. It had strengthened Patrick's resolve to fight, to truly fight, and he was hoping they would run into regular troops—perhaps Kansans—in their drive for Texas.

After the brothers had messed together that morning, they set about getting Frank outfitted. Zachary traded Lieutenant David

Poole the officer's jacket for a homespun coat, and Patrick found Frank a mount from among the Yankee horses that had been taken on the last raid. Zachary gave him two of the six Colt revolvers he carried, and when Frank loaded them using full charges Zachary shook his head.

"That's twice as much powder as you need," Zachary said. "Use twenty grains, at the most. It will kill a man just as dead, but there won't be enough kick to spoil your next shot. Powder can get scarce in the heat of a fight, and you need to make it last as long as possible."

Zachary also showed him how to use tallow from a lighted candle to seal the percussion caps upon the nipples and prevent moisture from fouling the powder, which would surely happen if they were forced to ride for more than a few hours in the rain.

"I never saw any action in St. Louis," Frank said apologetically. "I don't know how I'll be in the thick of it. I've never seen the elephant, Zach."

"Hell, Frank," Zachary said, "we *are* the elephant."

27

October 1863

THE FORAGING PARTY crossed Spring River at a rocky shoal and proceeded along the opposite bank toward Baxter Springs. The day was cold and bright and the trees along the river were showing touches of red and gold. Zachary was in the lead, his black cloak about his shoulders and the harness bells keeping rhythm to Raven's hoofbeats. Frank and Patrick were riding on his flank. The forty riders in Zachary's squad had been traversing the banks of the river, looking for food, but most of the cabins they came upon were deserted. Zachary decided to draw closer to the little settlement in hopes of finding better pickings.

Much had changed since the brothers had bought the cattle from the Universalist preacher John Baxter in the winter of '59. Baxter had been killed in a dispute with a renter over a piece of land and his family had scattered to Texas. The federals had thrown up an earth-and-logs fort along the spring that ran through the little community, but there was seldom more than a handful of soldiers at Fort Blair. Zachary reined to a halt on a hill overlooking the stream, and he motioned for the men to be quiet while he surveyed the situation.

Outside the fort a company of the Second Kansas Colored Infantry was preparing the midday meal over huge cooking pots. It smelled like stew to Zachary. Inside the earthworks the Third Wisconsin Cavalry was scattered about, repairing their tack or polishing their sabers or any one of the dozens of chores that went with life as a trooper. In the center of the fortifications, beside a lunette—a type of free-standing blockhouse—squatted a small howitzer on stout wheels.

"If it wasn't for that damned cannon," Zachary told Frank in a low voice, "I believe we would have some stew for lunch."

"That six-pounder does tend to spoil my appetite," Frank said.

Suddenly there was the thunder of hooves and pistols cracking as David Poole lead a charge from the tree line. The black troops abandoned their cooking pots and made for the safety of the earthworks as the guerrillas swept down upon them, and a handful fell in the dirt before their guns.

"Poole is a lunatic," Patrick said, but he was spurring his horse down the hill with the others as Zachary's squad spontaneously surged forward to bolster the assault.

"We'll have to get over those walls to take that fort," Zachary yelled, pulling his revolver and following the others. The squad rolled down the hill in a cacophony of creaking leather, pounding hooves, and Rebel yells. They reached the bottom of the hill, splashed through the spring, and galloped toward the fort.

Poole's men were beginning to waver as the soldiers formed behind the breastworks and put up a barrage of rifle fire. Two of them fell from their saddles, one landing dead in a cook fire. Zachary's squad raced through their milling ranks and, with pistols cracking, rushed the walls of the fort.

Quantrill's main force of two hundred and fifty was scattered in the hardwood along the river to the east of the fort when his scouts reported that a wagon train escorted by a hundred Union troops was moving down the military road from Fort Scott. He had been gathering his men to join in the skirmish he heard shaping up at the fort, and now he ordered the men to form a line to challenge the advancing Yankees.

General James G. Blunt, commander of the District of the Frontier, was on his way to Fort Gibson in the Indian Nations. Blunt saw the advancing line across the prairie and believed it to be an honor guard sent out from Fort Blair to receive him. He placed his colors and the wagon carrying his regimental band out front, and the brass struck up a parade tune. By the time the riders were close enough for Blunt to see they only partially wore blue—a stolen uniform here and there—it was too late. At sixty yards it was apparent that Quantrill and his band were bearing down upon them with reins held in their teeth or looped over saddle horns, carrying a pistol in each hand, the wind pressing the brims of their slouch hats back. As they closed they began hammering like devils.

The train disintegrated as the teamsters frantically turned their wagons, troopers bolted in every direction, and Blunt abandoned his buggy in favor of the closest horse at hand. Dozens of men were shot from their saddles as the raiders overtook them, and the rear made dash toward the ford at Willow Creek. Wagons overturned, teams collided, and riders were thrown in the confusion on the creek bank. A cannon and caisson cartwheeled down the muddy incline and disappeared in the water. Those that found themselves on foot were soon trampled down or shot.

Of the hundred men in the command, only twenty-two—including Blunt—escaped across the prairie. The rest lay scattered across the field among the band instruments and the broken supply wagons and an abandoned ambulance. Blunt's adjutant lay dead and his official correspondence, including his commissions, blew in the wind.

The guerrillas picked through the dead, taking money and jewelry and boots, and many of the corpses were stripped of their clothes. Blue uniforms were proving increasingly useful. Quantrill believed that one of the dead officers was Blunt himself, but there was no one left to correct him.

Patrick was the first to top the earthworks and he shot the closest trooper in the chest and sent a ball through the shoulder of another who was leveling a carbine at him. The others scattered for the cover of the lunette when Patrick was joined by a half-dozen other howling guerrillas on top of the mound of logs and earth.

The revolver shots came so quickly that it sounded like a string of firecrackers on the Fourth of July. Three more of the troopers sank mortally wounded to the earth. The rest of the squad began to pour over the earthworks. The guerrillas were on the verge of taking the fort.

In desperation a lieutenant dashed with two men from the door of the lunette to the howitzer. One man grasped the tongue of the carriage up and turned it upon the axle until the barrel pointed at the knot of guerrillas. The other spun the iron wheel beneath the breech to bring the muzzle down, but was shot in the face and fell backward. The lieutenant took his place, finished reducing the elevation until the bore was level with the earth, and ordered the other man to clear away. He snapped the firing lanyard from the vent.

The cannon roared smoke and fire. The earthworks erupted beneath the guerrillas and men and horses were flung into the air. Patrick's horse was struck dead beneath him and he pitched, stunned, to the ground inside what was left of the wall. The sulfurous smoke from the cannon lay like a blanket over the interior of the fort, providing cover for the besieged troopers, and the lieutenant struggled to reload the howitzer while his men dashed forward.

Blood ran from Patrick's nose and ears as he sat dazed upon the ground, his disemboweled horse beside him. Patrick could see crouching forms advancing through the smoke, but he could not get it clear in his mind what he should do or where his pistols had gone. If only he could get rid of the damned ringing in his ears, he thought, he could get things straight.

Zachary and Frank leapt from their horses side-by-side over the ruins of the wall as the first of the soldiers materialized through the smoke. Carbines and revolvers popped at the same time. Both of the guns in Frank's hands blazed as Zachary reached a hand down to Patrick.

Patrick looked up at him stupidly.

"God damn," Zachary said. Sliding from Raven's saddle to the ground, he shot a trooper who had his rifle against Patrick's head.

Frank wheeled his horse and dashed in front of his brothers to provide some cover. With three quick shots he discouraged a new wave of soldiers from breaking through.

"Haste!" Frank shouted. "You still don't want to die, do you?" His revolvers were snapping on empty cylinders.

"Dying's easy," Zachary said, tossing Frank one of his own guns. "Living's the hard part."

The howitzer spat again. Mud and stones rained down from a new hole in the wall, and billows of black smoke rolled over them.

Patrick was unable to get to his feet, so Zachary slung him over his shoulder and threw him across Raven's saddle. Zachary slapped Raven on the flank, but the horse refused to leave.

"Hang on," Zachary told Patrick.

Zachary pulled his remaining revolver, held it close to the

horse's head, and fired. Raven bolted away, bells ringing. Through the smoke Frank heard the familiar sound of Zachary's horse as it raced for cover, and Frank turned his horse and followed after.

The soldiers were again pushing forward. Zachary scrambled to make it over the wall, firing his revolver behind him, his boots slipping in the mud. Minié balls splattered around him. His right leg went out from beneath him and he fell heavily. He thought he had stumbled until he rolled over and saw the blood pouring from a shattered knee.

His last revolver was empty and he flung it at the advancing soldiers. He began to crawl, his fingers tearing desperately at the earth, dragging his useless leg behind him. He lay still when he felt the muzzle of a rifle press between his shoulder blades.

The shooting had stopped. The soldiers had retaken the fort and the guerrillas had galloped away into the timber. Nine Union soldiers were dead and a dozen wounded. Three dead guerrillas lay around and upon the broken wall.

"What are you waiting for?" Zachary asked, pounding his fist into the ground. "I'm not going to beg. I gave no quarter and expect none. Shoot me."

Zachary looked over his shoulder into the face of the black soldier holding the Enfield. It was Ben, the runaway slave that Frank had helped escape.

"My Lord," Ben said.

"What is it?" the lieutenant asked. His saber was out and he was directing the men into a skirmish line in case the guerrillas returned.

"Sir, this boy's family carried me over the line to freedom before the war," Ben said. "I can't kill him."

The lieutenant looked down at Zachary. His hands were covered with mud and powder smoke and he wore a cloak that was stained from months of campaigning. The boy's hard blue eyes met the lieutenant's, but they sought no appeal.

"He's an outlaw," the lieutenant said. "He led that last charge against us, and I believe he killed more of our men than any of the others. He will hang."

Zachary nodded his understanding.

"You fought right well," Zachary told the lieutenant. "If you had not had the sand to turn that cannon on us, I believe we would have taken this fort."

"I believe you would have," the lieutenant conceded.

"You ain't from Kansas, are you?"

"No," he said. "Wisconsin."

"That's good. I am glad that it was not a Kansan that got the best of me," Zachary said.

28

A<small>T DAWN</small> Zachary was hung without ceremony from a gnarled elm tree that stood beside the military road where it crossed the clear-water spring. When he was asked if he had anything to say for himself, Zachary shook his head. He had thought of asking them to tell Jennison he would see him in hell, but he did not want his last thought to be one of hate. Instead he looked toward the brilliant sunrise and thought of Sarah, and something within his thawing heart told him that their love had survived. Then the soldiers slapped the flank of the cavalry nag on which Zachary sat and he was free of the earth.

The soldiers left Zachary's body swinging in the breeze as a warning to others. For hours the blood ran down his leg and dripped from the tip of his right boot onto the ground. After the sun had set two riders came in the darkness and cut the body free of the rope.

They carried the body to the prairie near Willow Creek, where Blunt's overturned ambulance had not yet been recovered. Although Quantrill and company were by now deep in the Cherokee Nation, the detachment at the fort still feared attack. The men righted the vehicle and made a makeshift repair of one of the wheels and made a team of their horses. They wrapped the body in canvas and carefully laid it in the back of the ambulance. Then they climbed up into the seat and headed north.

The men wore ill-fitting blue uniforms with bloodstains on the back and revolvers tucked inside the jackets. Once they were stopped by a Union patrol. The patrol leader said the ambulance looked rather in need of repair and asked why they were carrying a dead man in the back.

"We're from Baxter Springs and this ambulance was beaten up when Quantrill took Blunt," the older man explained. A soldier was poking his head in the back of the ambulance. "Say, I wouldn't get too close to that one. The man died of infectious cardiac augury."

"I've never heard of that," the patrol leader said.

"It's very rare and very contagious," the man said. "Once it breaks out it's nearly impossible to control. It devastated Ireland in the seventeenth century. We're taking him back to the surgeons in Kansas City, and if the disease is confirmed, he'll be cremated. You can't bury the poor devils, you know."

"I see," the patrol leader said, backing his horse away. "Corpsmen, tell me something—if this disease is so dangerous, aren't you two worried that you'll catch it?"

The driver, the younger of the two, grinned. "We'd rather take our chances instead of being sent back south and meeting up with that devil Quantrill," he said.

"Carry on," the soldier said.

The men touched the brim of their hats and the ambulance rattled away. Two days later, the brothers would reach Cass County.

It took hours to dig the grave with their knives and boards taken from the ambulance, and when they were finished it was nearly daylight. Beside the long open hole was another grave, still mounded with dirt that the grass had not yet covered. A pile of rocks held a wooden cross upright with Sarah's name written in charcoal upon it.

"We'll come back, someday," Frank said as he carefully lowered the shoulders of the body into the grave and Patrick held the feet. "Then we'll put up a proper headstone for both of them."

They used boards to scoop the dirt back into the hole, and Patrick found a large flat stone and laid it at the head of the grave. He held a pebble in the palm of his hand and scratched an inscription: ZACHARY FENN, 1844–1863. Then Patrick added: RODE WITH QUANTRELL.

"Shouldn't we say something over him?" Patrick asked.

"I wouldn't know what to say," Frank replied. "That preacher trash would sound pretty weak right now."

"All I know to say is that he was our brother and that we loved him," Patrick said. "He was a true fellow and a good boy to ride with. He saved my life."

The birds were making a racket in the trees as the first light shot over the timber.

"Perhaps I do have something," Frank said, and took a piece of paper from his pocket. It was a page torn from a book, folded and smeared with fingerprints, and he had found it on Zachary after they had cut him down from the elm. On one side was a rather long poem called "Annabel Lee," but Frank believed it was the shorter poem, on the other side, that had prompted Zachary to keep the page.

Frank began to read.

The poem was short and ended with:

"And, as his strength failed him at length, he met a pilgrim shadow— 'Shadow,' said he, 'Where can it be—this land of Eldorado?'

"'Over the Mountains of the Moon, Down the Valley of the Shadow, ride, boldly ride,' the shade replied, 'if you seek for Eldorado!'"

Frank climbed into the seat beside Patrick, who held the reins. It was full daylight and Frank looked around him uncomfortably.

"Now what?" Patrick asked.

"I don't know," Frank said. "We've been damn lucky so far and I'm afraid to push that luck. We need to hide ourselves until dark, but there's not a barn left standing within twenty miles. Any ideas?"

Patrick rested his chin in his hands.

"What about Amarugia?" he asked suddenly. "We're an hour away, and Cole Younger told me that he and the James brothers hid from the Yankees there before. There's plenty of caves and other places to hide deep in the hollow."

"It is worth a try," Frank said.

"Maybe we should saddle the horses," Patrick suggested. "I feel like we draw attention to ourselves in this meat wagon."

"Not as much attention as two armed riders in uniforms that don't fit," Frank said. "We wouldn't get ten miles before a patrol shot us out of the saddle. At least with the ambulance we don't look like a threat. Let's keep it a spell."

Patrick nodded and flicked the reins.

29

THE AMBULANCE rattled down the rutted trail that snaked through the hollow. When they reached the clearing near the creek they found the shacks that had surrounded Basby Owens' court were burned to the ground and his ruined throne lying among the ashes.

"I reckon Basby found somebody stronger than him at last," Patrick said.

They drove the ambulance through the ruins and down to the creek, searching for a suitable cave among those that dotted the bluff. They were crossing the shallow creek to the other side when they spotted a dark-haired girl kneeling at the edge of the water, beating clothes upon a rock. She looked up and saw the wagon and the two blue-coated men. Patrick thought he knew her, and when he spotted the gleam of a knife in her belt when she turned to run he was sure.

Patrick stood up in the seat.

"Trudy!" he shouted.

The girl stopped and stared.

"Patrick?" she asked, taking a few steps toward them. Then she broke into a run and splashed her way across the creek. Patrick jumped down from the seat, swept her up in his arms, and whirled with her.

"I was afraid you'd never come back," Trudy said. He kissed her and she lay her head against his shoulder and looked up at Frank.

"Frank," she said excitedly, and grasped his hand. She pulled him down and led him across the stream to a mound of brush.

Behind the brush was a cavern, and sitting on a wooden box in the center of the cavern near the fire was Jenny, and beside her was Little Frank.

"My God," Frank said. "You're alive."

They embraced and Jenny whispered a prayer of thanks. Then Frank picked up the child and held him in the air and looked in wonder at him.

"I came back to the farm," Frank explained. "I found bones in the ashes—"

"Fitz," Jenny said. "He tried to keep them from burning the house. He swore he would never let another Yank—another Union soldier set foot on the place."

Frank closed his eyes.

"Trudy found me on the road the night after Jennison came, and she brought me here and has taken care of us since. Trudy is a wonderful woodsman and has seen to it that we have had plenty of fish and game. She kept telling me all along that you would come for me."

They kissed.

"Frank," she asked. "Where have you been?"

"It's a rather long story," he said. "I am an outlaw now."

"Quantrill," she said without emotion.

Frank quickly told her about his desertion from the army, how the brothers had planned to make for Texas, and what had happened at the fight at Baxter Springs. He told her that Zachary had been hung and that the promise to bury him next to Sarah had been kept.

"Texas," Jenny said. "Is there fighting there?"

"It is not like here," Frank said.

"Don't leave us," she said.

"It will be dangerous," Frank said.

"Promise you will take us," she said. "You can't leave us again, Frank. I would simply lie down and die. Take us to Texas with you and let us make a new home far away from Jennison and the rest."

"I won't leave you," Frank said.

Trudy looked nervously at her hands.

"We can't leave Trudy," Jenny said quickly. "She can't stay in this cave for the winter. She must come with us."

"Oh, I can't leave Amarugia," Trudy said lightly. "I'm used to the woods and I would scare regular folks—"

"Come with us," Patrick said, grasping her hand. "I wouldn't have it any other way, not after what you've done for Jenny and Little Frank. And I reckon we can find a preacher somewhere along the way, if you will have me."

30

THE ROAD out of Cass County took them through the Little Shannon Valley and past the lane that led to the lonely chimney on the side of the hill. Patrick had not seen the farm since Jennison had burned it and he implored Frank to stop the ambulance for a moment, but Frank was unsure.

"Let him say goodbye," Jenny suggested.

Frank turned the ambulance up the lane and reined the horses to a halt in the yard. Patrick stood among the blackened timbers for a few minutes, until Frank called out to him.

"There is trouble coming up the lane," Frank said. "I think you had better climb back up here and be prepared to story or fight."

Patrick walked as casually as he could muster back to the ambulance while the half-dozen Union soldiers, followed by a buggy, rode up to the ruins of the house. A captain and a woman with a bundle on her lap sat in the buggy.

"What are you snooping about for?" a corporal demanded as he approached the ambulance. "Where are you from and what is your business here?"

"We're with the third Wis—"

"Your uniforms are filthy. What's the sign and the countersign, or don't you even know it?"

The buggy pulled into the yard. Caitlin sat in the seat beside the federal captain, and her eyes went wide with horror as she recognized that it was Frank and Patrick the corporal was questioning.

The battle at Baxter Springs and the slaughter of Blunt's men had plunged the border into another state of readiness, and Ewing's headquarters had received with grim satisfaction the news that the guerrilla Zachary Fenn had been captured and executed. Captain Blake, who had arrested Caitlin and felt partially responsible for the ham-fisted manner in which the guerrillas' women had been dealt with, quickly appealed that there was no longer any justification for holding Caitlin because Zachary was dead. Upon her release from the women's barracks Blake was waiting for her with a buggy, and Ewing and the rest could be damned if they didn't like it. Caitlin had said she wanted to be taken to find Sarah's mother at Trading Post.

"What's the sign?" the corporal demanded again.

"There's been so dogged many of them lately," Patrick said, and casually stuck his hand inside his shirt and scratched his stomach. His fingers were just a few inches from the butt of his revolver.

"What's the trouble?" Blake asked.

"These men, sir," the corporal said. "They appear not to know the sign or even to be able to tell us who they are."

Blake stepped down from the buggy and walked over to the ambulance. He looked at the ragged uniforms and their dirty hands and at their blue eyes and he knew they were Caitlin's brothers.

"What's wrong with you men?" Blake asked. "The sign is, 'Lyon is sleeping,' and the countersign is, 'Step lightly then.' You have arrived somewhat early. I did not expect you for another hour."

"Sir?" Frank asked.

"But I assume the lady is ready. She requested one last look at her home before continuing south."

Caitlin handled the bundle over to Blake as she stepped awkwardly out of the carriage. Within the bundle was a sleeping baby. Caitlin's right leg ended at the knee, and only one foot could be seen as she reached the ground. Blake handed her a pair of crutches from the buggy, and he followed behind her with the baby.

"You men go on down the hill and leave Miss Fenn a moment's peace while she looks over what's left of the family home," Blake commanded. The corporal shook his head but touched a finger to the brim of his hat and led the men back down the hill.

"I don't know why you have done this for me," Caitlin said as she leaned against the ambulance and took the baby from him. "You Yankees are all a mystery to me."

"I am not sure that I can explain it myself," Blake said and took off his hat. "I hope that you will find it in your heart to forgive me and allow me to write to you after the war."

"I do not think that would be appropriate," Caitlin said stiffly. Blake flushed.

"I understand," he said. Then he looked up at the brothers. "You must give me your word that you will make no trouble until you are out of my district. God help all of us if you ever come back."

Blake stepped into the buggy, tipped his hat to Caitlin, and turned the horse back down the lane. Frank watched as he met up with the soldiers, and they rode away together. When they were out of sight they opened the back of the ambulance and lifted Caitlin and the baby into it.

"My God, aren't you going to ask?" Caitlin said.

"There's nothing to explain," Frank said. "We are just glad to see you again."

"No!" Caitlin said. "You don't understand. The baby is *Sarah's*. She gave birth to her in prison, six months ago, but she was so ashamed because she and Zachary weren't married that she made me promise not to tell anyone. Then, after she was killed, there wasn't anybody I could get word to any longer."

"She's beautiful," Patrick said, touching her cheek. "She looks like both of them."

"Her name is Annabel," Caitlin said.

"Can I hold her?" Trudy asked.

Caitlin looked at her suspiciously, remembering the days before the war, but she softened when Patrick took the baby and placed her in Trudy's arms.

Jenny hugged Caitlin, and told her how much she had missed her, and she showed her the family Bible that she had thrown in her grain sack before Jennison burned the house.

Caitlin took the Bible and held it in her lap. She ran her hand over the cover, then opened it to where the births and deaths and marriages were recorded in the front.

"We have some catching up to do," Caitlin remarked.

Frank's eyes misted and he turned away so the others would not see. Patrick squeezed Trudy's shoulders and Jenny held Little Frank a little more tightly.

"We're a family again," Patrick said. Then he jumped down

from the ambulance and walked to the edge of the ruined house. He looked at the debris for a moment, then he glanced toward the graves on the hill.

"You know, I reckon Pa was wrong," Patrick said. "It's not the land that's important—it's us. *We* are what counts. They can take the land away from us, and burn our homes, and trample our crops—they can even kill us—but they will never be able to change what we feel for each other. They will never be able to take away the memories—of Pa and Fitz, Sarah, and Zachary. Especially Zachary. As long as we live, he lives."

Frank reached a hand down to him.

"Come on, brother," Frank said. "Let's go home."

About the Author

Max McCoy is an award-winning journalist and native Kansan. *The Sixth Rider,* his previous Double D Western, received the Western Writers of America's Medicine Pipe Bearer's Award for best first novel of the year.

W
McCoy, Max
Sons of fire